The man raised his rifle and aimed it at Dane, Josie and Everly.

Dane pulled Everly into his grasp as he dived for cover. They rolled underneath thick foliage.

As shots lit up the night, he looked for Josie. She was already on the ground, propped up on her elbows with her pistol in her grip. She didn't take her eyes off the shooter as she fired two rounds.

The guy shot once more before he turned and barreled into the foliage.

Josie stood up and rushed forward. "Are you okay, honey? Were you hurt?"

"I'm not hurt." Everly climbed to her knees and clung to her collie as she sobbed.

"Let's go back to the cabin, pack up and go home." Josie motioned with her hand.

"It won't matter. That man is going to kill me."

"Everly, no." Josie moved to her side. "I won't let anyone hurt you."

"The man will kill you like he did my daddy. We're all going to die because of me!"

Connie Queen has spent her life in Texas, where she met and married her high school sweetheart. Together they've raised eight children and are enjoying their grandchildren. Today, as an empty nester, Connie lives with her husband and her Great Dane, Nash, and is working on her next suspense novel.

Books by Connie Queen

Love Inspired Suspense

Visit the Author Profile page at LoveInspired.com.

Wilderness Witness Survival

CONNIE QUEEN

LOVE INSPIRED SUSPENSE
INSPIRATIONAL ROMANCE

LOVE INSPIRED® SUSPENSE
INSPIRATIONAL ROMANCE

ISBN-13: 978-1-335-59963-6

Wilderness Witness Survival

Copyright © 2024 by Connie Queen

Recycling programs for this product may not exist in your area.

This is a work of fiction. Names, characters, places and incidents are either the product of the author's imagination or are used fictitiously. Any resemblance to actual persons, living or dead, businesses, companies, events or locales is entirely coincidental.

For questions and comments about the quality of this book, please contact us at CustomerService@Harlequin.com.

® is a trademark of Harlequin Enterprises ULC.

Love Inspired
22 Adelaide St. West, 41st Floor
Toronto, Ontario M5H 4E3, Canada
www.LoveInspired.com

Printed in Lithuania

MIX
Paper | Supporting responsible forestry
FSC® C021394

And whoso shall receive one such little child
in my name receiveth me.
—*Matthew* 18:5

To my wonderful partner in crime, Sharee Stover,
who joins me every day to write. For all the
that's-not-how-that-works and the "unique" ways
of answering the what-ifs, I thank you.
You're a great friend and make the journey more fun.

ONE

From this day forward, Everly Caroline Hunt is your child to have. Congratulations! The memory of balloons, coworkers clapping, and Judge Torbett handing his gavel to eight-year-old Everly to slam on his desk in celebration of the adoption evaporated in the muggy Texas night air.

How could Josie Hunt's dreams of being a mom go so wrong in only four months of parenthood?

Fear ran through her veins as she took another step into the dark woods wearing hiking boots. Had her daughter really run away? At ten thirty at night, no less. She called again, "Everly!"

Only silence greeted her.

She couldn't have gone far. Josie had planned this weekend vacation to the secluded cabin, believing it would help her and Everly bond. A little fun with no worries. S'mores by a campfire and taking daily hikes while admiring nature type of thing.

Evidently not.

The first chance her daughter had gotten, she'd

taken off. Maybe Josie should've sensed something was wrong. Everly had been even quieter than normal after they stopped to pick up pizza at a hole-in-the-wall place on the outskirts of the boonies. Josie had chalked it up to being tired after the drive, but now she wondered if her daughter had been making her plans to run.

But why? Was Josie really that bad of a mom?

The eight-year-old had been left an orphan when her dad, an acquaintance of Josie's, died in a tragic home accident a few months ago—a fall into the hot tub while trimming the grass with an electric trimmer and he was electrocuted. Everly's mom died of a rare heart disorder when the girl was a toddler. Josie had dreamed of having a family for a long time, but out of the guys she'd dated, one had let her down by getting into trouble with the law and the other had been mainly interested in a career. Family was important and there was no room to put a child on the back burner. How could she give a romantic relationship a chance if he wasn't a family man?

Josie had jumped at the chance to adopt the sweet girl, seeing there weren't family members willing to take Everly in. Even though normally there was a six-month waiting period to adopt in Texas, the judge waived the time because her parents were deceased, and he was familiar with Josie.

But being a competent investigator with the

sheriff's department and for the Bring the Children Home Project—a volunteer organization of professionals who worked with law enforcement to help find missing children—had not prepared Josie for motherhood.

A footstep sounded behind her. Just as Josie started to turn, a powerful arm wrapped around her collarbone from behind. The sharp tip of a knife bit into the side of her neck. "Where is your daughter?"

She froze. *Oh, Lord. Please help me!* Who is this man? Her Sig rested out of reach in her ankle holster as the man pulled her against his chest. Being that she was five feet eight and her shoulders came to his chest meant he must be over six feet tall. "I don't know."

"If you want to live, you better start talking." The hoarse male voice held a drawl, which meant he was probably a local.

The last time she'd seen her daughter was when Everly went to bed with Dexter, her border collie. The next thing Josie knew, she was awakened by Dexter's sharp bark from somewhere outside. Everly's window was open, and her daughter and dog were gone. Josie had grabbed her weapon and cell phone and stepped into the night calling her name. A lump in Josie's throat grew, making it difficult to swallow, the blade digging deeper. "I don't know," she repeated. "She's gone."

The man hesitated.

Did he believe her? Or was he contemplating slashing her throat? One thing was certain, she had to get away from him to find her daughter.

"You're going to help me find her."

No, I'm not. Defense training kicked in, and she held up her hands as if in surrender. She said, "Okay. Okay." As soon as his hold relaxed, she shifted her hip, and in one swift move, grabbed his right wrist with both hands and yanked downward. His arm bent over her shoulder, hyperextending his elbow.

He dropped the knife and cursed.

She took off through the woods at a sprint, dodging trees. As she leaped over a fallen branch, her knee almost buckled when she landed, but she kept going several more yards before stopping to retrieve her Sig from her holster.

"You're going to pay for that!" the man called. Snapping twigs told her he was coming for her.

Keeping her weapon in her grip, she took off again, but this time at a quieter, slower pace. She could've shot at him, but she couldn't take the chance since she didn't know Everly's location. Her mind scrambled with what the guy wanted as she weaved through the brush in search of Everly. If she and Dexter were close by, surely the dog would've barked.

The vacation cabin she'd rented sat on over twenty-five acres. Since Dexter's barking had awakened her, the two couldn't be that far ahead. Unless Everly had gone in the opposite direction.

Her daughter didn't own a cell phone, but as Josie moved deeper into the woods, she thought of calling Bliss, her boss at Bring the Children Home Project. Not slowing down, she reached into the pocket on her shorts, but the Velcro was no longer fastened. Her phone was gone. She must've dropped it while wrestling with the guy.

Was there more than one attacker? Had someone kidnapped Everly? Working with Bring the Children Home Project tended to make her believe every child was a potential kidnapping victim. Her stomach knotted at the thought.

Everly was a timid child. Surely, she wouldn't have run this far. Josie must've gone the wrong way. She was about to switch course when something shiny dangling in the brush grabbed her attention. It was Everly's pink butterfly necklace that her daddy had given her on her last birthday.

Jose untangled it from the limb and noticed the chain was broken. She shoved it into her pocket.

"Everly. Are you here?" She kept her voice down, but maybe the girl had stopped to hide. "Honey, it's me. Come out if you hear me."

When she received no answer, she picked her way through the woods again. Every few seconds, she looked over her shoulder to see if the tall man had closed in on her.

The longer she went, the more her heart raced

with disbelief that the eight-year-old had run this far. She picked up the pace and trekked the uneven ground, watching for more signs Everly had gone this way. If she didn't locate her soon, she'd hurry back to where she thought she had lost her phone. Then she'd call the authorities and her team to help search for her and, hopefully, to arrest the man who'd pulled the knife on her.

"Everly," she called again. Frustration settled in.

Black shadows blended into the trees, making it almost impossible to see. The toe of her running shoe hung on a limb and caused her to fall hard. Dirt and gravel bit into her hands as pain radiated through her. She climbed back to her feet and dusted her hands on her legs before taking off again at a fast walk. A frog croaked somewhere, and crickets chirped.

Crash.

Josie jerked at the sound that came from behind her and to the left as she searched for the source. In the opposite direction, a dog barked. That had to be Dexter.

She came to a clearing and listened.

A branch snapped. This time the noise was closer, as if the source was on the move. "Everly. Is that you?" No response. "If you're out here, please answer me."

More popping and rustling came from the woods.

She switched her Sig to her other hand while wiping the sweat away, before transferring the weapon again to her shooting hand. Hunching low, she wove her way through the brush.

A bulky shadow presented itself against an oak. She froze. Her breath hitched as she concentrated on making out the silhouette, and she stayed low. Being that the man had been behind her when he'd pulled the knife, she hadn't gotten a clear look at him.

A child's scream sounded in the darkness. *Everly!*

Suddenly, the shadow vanished. She blinked, trying to clear her vision. There were only the trees.

With her gun ready, she hurried to the oak. Nothing.

She took off, determined to find her daughter before the man did. Snaking through the woods, she heard water running like that from a creek.

Another scream sent chills down Josie's neck.

Even though the darkness hung like a black, impassable curtain, she dashed through the trees. Something cracked to her right, but she kept going.

She'd been in dangerous situations before. Exchanged gunfire. Helped rescue children. But Everly was *her* child.

Gripping her gun tighter, she mentally prepared for the unknown.

* * *

Dane Haggerty moved through the woods, crouched low as he maneuvered the tunnel-like trail in search of what sounded like a girl's scream. There was nothing for miles except for wilderness and wild animals. At first, he'd thought the scream might be that of a mountain lion, but he was certain it was that of a child.

His flashlight remained on his belt until he found out what had made the noise. If there was a child out here, he could only guess he or she was lost.

"Everly," a lady's voice called.

Dane stopped in his tracks and automatically pulled the baseball cap down further on his head. Did he dare take the chance of being found now? Maybe he should return to his hideout since an adult—probably the parent—was nearby.

But it wasn't in him not to help someone in trouble, even if there was a warrant for his arrest.

A dog yipped somewhere close.

A growl rose on the wind. As the heavy grunts grew louder, he tried to place the animal.

The growl didn't come from a dog or a wild pig.

A terrifying scream provoked him to move. He clicked on his flashlight and took off again. As he came out in a clearing on the edge of a creek bank, an ominous black shadow moved in the night.

The girl's cries were pure terror. He moved closer and aimed the flashlight. The outline of a burly bear with his nose on the inside of a fallen tree trunk was illuminated from the shadows.

The child's squeals came from inside the rotted wooden log.

Ignoring the dangerous predicament, he moved in and yelled, "Get back." He removed his Glock from his holster, although he doubted it was powerful enough to stop the animal from mauling him should it attack.

The black bear suddenly looked up, his nose pointing upward, and gave a horrifying growl.

"Go on. Get away from there." Dane stood tall and waved the light again. "Get."

The bear swung his head and snarled.

Dane had never been confronted by a bear, but as the child cried out again, he took another step forward, putting him within twenty feet of the beast. He looked around. If the animal charged, he'd have no place to hide except to take a chance of jumping into the creek and hoping he could move fast enough to escape.

The bear looked back at the hollow log and then ran off into the trees, disappearing.

Dane hurried forward and pointed his light inside the open end of the trunk. A young girl with braids huddled in the far end with her arms wrapped around a dog. "The bear is gone. You can come out now."

Large, tearful eyes stared back, and she shook her head vehemently.

"Where is your family?" She must have been scared to death. How did she get separated from her parents? Especially at this time of night. When she didn't answer, he said, "My name is Dane. I live right over there." He pointed to the north. "I will not hurt you. I have a cell phone where we can call your parents." As soon as the words were out, he regretted them. How could he help her and keep his identity hidden at the same time? Tears continued to flow down her cheeks. "I know you must be frightened, but I assure you the bear is gone."

A huff-like growl came from the trees, making the fluffy dog bark.

This was not a good time for the animal to return. "We need to go. I'm climbing in to get you."

"No." She held up her hand.

"Look, the bear is gone, but he's still moving around in the woods. We need to get you out of there." *Please, Lord, help her not panic and run.* He went down on all fours and crawled into the dark, musty log.

"No!" The girl held her hand out.

"I'm trying to help you. The bear is coming back. Come on." He pumped his hands closed, indicating she should move to him now.

The snarl came from somewhere close, and the girl didn't fight when Dane scooped her into his arms and backed out of the log. The collie crawled out after them. When Dane got to his feet, he spotted the bear moving through the trees. Quickly, he fired a shot into a nearby tree, hoping to scare the animal away. The beast hesitated.

Dane wasted no time stuffing his gun in the back of his waistband and heading in the opposite direction, with the girl in his grasp and the dog at his feet. He weaved in and out of the brush.

"Everly," a woman's voice called. "Where are you?"

"Mom!"

A lady wearing a pink T-shirt and shorts would've run into him if he hadn't come to a halt.

"Give me my daughter. Now." Shadows hid her features.

She held her hands out to the girl, but Dane pulled her back. "No time. There's a bear out here, and we need to move now. It'll be faster if I carry her."

"There are no bears in north Texas."

Yeah, right. Without arguing, he continued through the trees, away from the animal. He didn't know if bears would track a man, but he wasn't taking any chances.

"Stop," the woman demanded. Moonlight glistened from the end of a gun barrel. "I'm armed."

"I can see that." Panting for breath, he stopped long enough to eye the pistol in her hand. Unless the darkness gave him cover, his scruffy beard, faded black T-shirt, cap, and holey jeans gave her the wrong impression. He put the girl on her feet. "Let's keep moving."

"Are you okay, Everly?"

The concern in the woman's voice wasn't lost on him. He wanted to ask why the girl would go wandering off by herself, but it wasn't his business. Sometimes kids did dumb things.

"I'm fine, Mom."

"We'll talk later." The lady turned on him. "Throw down your knife."

"I don't have a knife." He glanced around to make certain the bear hadn't followed them.

She continued with her pistol trained on him. "I won't ask again."

"Listen, lady. I don't know who you think I am, but I don't have a knife." Since he shot to scare the bear away, and she'd probably heard, he added, "I do have a gun, but I'm not giving it up. We need to get out of here. Come with me if you want."

He took off, hoping she wouldn't shoot him. What was wrong with the woman? Who did she mistake him for?

The two followed close behind him. Once they'd gone several hundred yards without seeing any signs of the bear, curiosity got the best of him. He glanced over his shoulder. "What are you doing out here? There's nothing around for miles."

Even in the dark, he was certain that was a frown. He tried not to look her straight on to keep his identity hidden.

"You're not fooling anyone, mister. But we'll get to the bottom of this." She paused. "I could ask you the same thing."

The woman sounded familiar. Not so much the voice, but the attitude when she talked. Being two hours from his stomping grounds, it was doubtful he knew her. What had she asked? What he was doing out here. He held his hands in the air. "I heard the girl calling for help."

She clipped, "I'm sure she was."

"Where are you staying?" There weren't many homes or people in the area. Being that it was night, the woman probably hadn't made out his features, but he didn't need anyone recognizing him. And he sure wouldn't compromise his hideout.

"I'm not certain. Maybe a half a mile to the south." She looked at him and their eyes met, causing him to freeze momentarily.

Josie Hunt? What were the chances of him meeting up with her in the middle of nowhere when he just happened to be wanted for murder? Not likely.

"My name's Josie and this is Everly."

Oh no. He still didn't believe it. She was the last person he wanted to see. He had to keep her from recognizing him if she hadn't already. "Let's get you back." Purposefully, he kept his voice low. He needed to keep moving, so he started back on the trail again and was glad when they followed. He glanced to the right and pointed. "That way."

"You don't have a vehicle?" Suspicion laced her voice.

He did, but he couldn't give away his identity. If possible, he needed to keep to the shadows of the trees so she couldn't make out his features. He'd stayed off the grid for four months. But he also didn't want to leave the two alone with a bear wandering the area. "I do."

Everly faced her mom. "I don't want to go back with you. I'll just run away again."

Her words had him taking another glance at the girl. What had made her run from Josie?

"Don't say that. I know you miss your daddy, but *we're* a family now." Josie turned to him. "We can find our way on our own." Josie ran her hand down Everly's braids in a comforting gesture, but the girl jerked away.

"I don't want to go back to the cabin or home."

The fear in the girl's voice was clear, and Dane was torn as to what to do. Had Josie been abusive? The woman he knew could never hurt a child. Maybe she had a violent husband or boyfriend. *I know you miss your daddy.* Had Josie's husband left her?

"I can protect you." Josie eyed her daughter.

"As soon as we make it back to the cabin, we'll get in our vehicle and go home."

"No!" Everly wrapped her arms around Dane's waist. "I want to go with him. I'm scared."

The girl's action rocked him, making him cringe. Even in the dark, the sharp prick of the daughter's words could be felt. He could relate to not wanting to go home as a child, but Josie was nothing like his family. She'd always been kind to him. Well, almost always. If you didn't count the time she turned him in to the police for theft—a crime that he didn't commit.

Clouds drifted away from the moon, causing the light to shine on their faces.

Josie's eyebrows scrunched as she looked at him. "You look familiar."

Purposefully, he took a step into the shadows and turned away. "I get that a lot."

Not only had he and Josie dated in high school—he didn't know if she even remembered him—but she'd been the one person in school to make him believe in himself and give him hope that he didn't have to follow in his father's footsteps. They'd only been teens, but her actions had meant everything to him—until she betrayed him. A pang in his heart still ached more than it should have. The last few months, his picture had been all over the news. The last thing he needed was Josie to blow his cover. If he had any intention of not going to prison for murder, he needed to escape these two now.

Framed for killing his business partner, Harlan Schmidt, Dane had been in hiding while trying to find evidence that exonerated him. Was he doomed to be incarcerated again? If authorities arrested him this time, he was certain he'd never see daylight again. He couldn't let that happen.

Not if he wanted to save Violet.

The court date for his thirteen-year-old sister to become a ward of the state was in less than three weeks. There was no one else in his family who could fight for her. He had worked tirelessly for a spotless reputation and to have a successful business. No one knew better than Dane how being raised not knowing where your next meal was coming from could cause you to make poor decisions.

Something rustled in the trees. All three of them turned toward the sound.

The girl wrapped her arms around his arm. "Don't let him take me."

"Stay close. I won't let the bear get you." Dane pulled her against him.

As he searched out the animal's location, movement caught his attention, and he realized the culprit's silhouette only had two legs and a rifle in his hands. Maybe he was a camper who'd heard Dane's shots.

Everly cried and moved behind Dane. "Don't let him hurt me."

Josie eyed her daughter.

The rifle must've frightened the girl, but Dane wanted the man to know they had shot to scare a dangerous animal. "We were warning off a bear. There's no need to be alarmed."

Suddenly, the man raised his rifle and aimed it at them.

A microsecond later, the attacker's intentions dawned on him, and Dane pulled Everly into his grasp as he dove for cover. They rolled underneath thick foliage.

As shots lit up the night, he looked for Josie. He and Josie warned in unison, "Get down."

But Josie was already on the ground, propped up on her elbows with her pistol in her grip. She didn't take her eyes off the shooter as she readied her aim and fired two rounds.

Dread filled him, as he didn't know what kind of trouble had followed his old high school sweetheart into the wilderness. Which also spelled trouble for him if it led authorities to his doorstep.

As the thoughts stabbed him like a thousand needles, he also realized he couldn't leave Josie and Everly's sides until he knew they were safe.

He slid his weapon from his waistband.

The guy shot once more before he turned and barreled into the foliage.

Everly buried her head under Dane's arm. "This is all my fault."

"No." Dane gave her a gentle squeeze. He didn't know how a kid could come to that conclusion, but she needed to understand. "This is not your fault."

Josie rushed forward. "Are you okay, honey? Were you hurt?"

"I'm not hurt." The girl's voice came out loud and frustrated. She climbed to her knees and clung to the collie as sobs racked her body.

"Let's go back to the cabin, pack up and go home." Josie motioned with her hand.

"You're not listening." Finally, she looked at her mom and shouted with tears in her eyes. "It won't matter. That man is going to kill me."

"Everly, no." Josie moved to her side. "I won't let anyone hurt you."

"The man will kill you like he did my daddy. We're all going to die because of me!"

The dog barked and danced at the girl's feet.

"Someone killed her dad?" Dane glanced from her to Josie as he returned his weapon to his waistband.

Josie shook her head and whispered, "Her father died in an accident."

"No." Everly balled her fists. "It was on purpose! I saw that man with the gun drown him in our hot tub. He held him under. The man's been following me ever since. He's watched me at school, and he was at the pizza place."

"Oh, baby. I will protect you." Josie wrapped her arms around the girl, and then she looked at Dane. "We're leaving and going straight to the sheriff's department."

Of course, Josie needed to go to the authorities. But what would she do when she recognized his identity? No doubt she'd turn him in. And he wouldn't blame her one bit.

His gaze went from Josie to the girl. "Come on. I'll see you safely back to your cabin." There was no way Dane would let Josie and Everly walk back alone when there was a killer after them.

TWO

Josie held her daughter, her heart breaking, while tuning out the stranger's comment about walking them back to the cabin. Her mind tried to sort through everything at a hundred miles per hour. She pulled back from the embrace and ran her hand over Everly's face and repeated, "No one is going to kill you or me. Do you understand?"

Her daughter's forehead wrinkled into a frown before the tears flowed freely. "Yes, he will. If Daddy couldn't stop him, neither can you."

A knife stabbed Josie in the heart. "Oh, baby. I'll do everything to keep you safe. Do you know the man's name?"

Everly shook her head. "No, but I got a good look at him. He went into the pizza place. That's why I ran. Please don't be mad. I was trying to find a place to hide and lead him away from you."

A lump formed in Josie's throat. She hugged her daughter once again as she tried to remember the people who had been in the store. The place was small and almost deserted. She simply hadn't paid attention to anyone except to the woman behind the counter. "I could never be mad at you. I wish I would've known."

"I'm sorry."

"Don't be. I'm glad you told me."

"Josie." The stranger's voice interrupted their moment. "We need to get moving. Now that we know who he's targeting, we don't need to be caught out here on foot. With him or the bear."

She wanted to console her daughter, but the stranger was right. "Let's go."

Dark shadows had kept her from making out the gunman's identity, but maybe when they got back to Liberty, Everly could identify the man from mug shots.

"There's still no sign of that guy. Let's get you two to safety."

Suspicions arose. Josie turned back to the trees where the guy had stood to make certain he was gone. Satisfied, she holstered her Sig into the largest pocket of her shorts and Velcroed it shut. She looked at the stranger and noticed he glanced away. "What are *you* doing out here?"

"I've already answered that. I heard your child scream."

Something wasn't right. Was this man in cahoots with the gunman? Possibly. If he was, at least she'd know where one man was. Right now, all she wanted was to get somewhere safe. She grasped Everly's hand without a word and they wove their way through the trees at a fast pace toward the cabin. If the gunman tried to circle around and get in front of them, he'd have to run.

Ten minutes later, they came to a trail, and the woods thinned. She stopped and turned to the stranger. "Who are you?"

She observed him. His dark eyes disappeared under that bib of his cap in the moonlight, and his scraggly beard covered most of his face. Her attention returned to the eyes. They were almost familiar.

He glanced down and stared at his feet. "Ma'am, I'd be glad to see you two back to wherever you're staying."

"And your name?"

"It's not important."

She gave him another look. Irritation crawled over her. The relationship with her daughter was not going as planned, and now someone was targeting them. If Everly was correct and she witnessed Pierce's murder, then the killer would need to dispose of her.

Josie wanted to dismiss the stranger but trekking through the woods had not been in a straight line and the darkness had prevented her from noticing landmarks. Stubbornness was something she struggled with, but she had Everly to consider. It was time to swallow her pride. "Are you familiar with the Hidden Oaks cabin?"

"Yes, ma'am. I know the location if that's what you're asking. I can lead you there."

The stranger's manners confused her. He appeared rough and unkempt in contrast to his speech. "That won't be necessary." She pointed to the right, which felt like the south. "Is it that way?"

"Yes, ma'am. If you stay on this trail, it's about a half mile to a metal walkthrough gate to the backyard of your place."

She wished he'd quit calling her ma'am. "I lost my cell phone back there. Can you call in the shooter to the sheriff's department?"

"I will let them know."

She held out her hand. "If you let me borrow your phone, I can call them now."

"It won't do any good. There's no reception out here. I'll call them in a bit."

She squinted. There was something about him she didn't trust. She wasn't about to let him lead them back to the cabin. They would pack and leave as quickly as possible. She rested a hand on Everly's shoulder and pulled her close in a protective gesture. "We don't need help."

He said, "Be careful."

She slipped into the darkness with her daughter's hand in hers. After they went several yards, she glanced back. The stranger was nowhere in sight.

Thankfully, Everly stayed close to her. As they

hiked down the rugged path, her mind kept returning to the stranger.

Where did he go? Was he camping in the woods? He claimed to hear Everly scream. Maybe. The most important question was what if he was working with the gunman.

They made tracks through the brush, hurrying toward their cabin with Dexter trotting happily at their side. After several minutes, Everly tugged on her hand, and Josie released her grip.

By the time they got back to the rental cabin, Josie was exhausted, and her feet ached. Nothing would be better than curling up in bed and getting a good night's rest, but sleep wasn't in her future.

Maybe she could reschedule this getaway in the summer after authorities found Pierce's killer and Everly visited with Kennedy, the psychologist for Bring the Children Home Project.

The back door was left unlocked from when Josie rushed outside to find Everly. She retrieved her gun from her pocket. Uncertainty whether she should have Everly wait outside or follow her inside nagged at her, but she decided on the latter. "Follow me and stay close."

They walked through the log structure together, including Everly's room, with Dexter at their side. By all appearances, nothing had been touched. As they stopped between the kitchen and living room, the border collie immediately lay at Everly's feet with his tail in rapid motion, slapping the wooden floor.

A smile crossed Josie's lips. "I think we're all tired." She turned back to Everly. "Pack your bag, and I'll get my things together. We'll leave in two minutes."

Everly went into her room, taking Dexter with her. She left the door wide open.

Sadness fell on Josie that Everly had witnessed such atrocities at such a young age. Hopefully, the girl would learn to trust her and could begin healing after her father's murderer was caught.

As she rushed to throw her clothes and toiletries into her bag, she wondered whether the authorities would believe Everly's story. At only eight, Everly could have easily misinterpreted what had happened. But Josie believed her. Being that she'd seen the man several times and that he'd followed them on their vacation told Josie the girl had not misunderstood.

Moonlight seeped into the cabin, making use of lights optional. The rustic home was in the middle of nowhere, but if someone was outside, they could easily see through the large floor-to-ceiling glass panes in the living room. The eerie feeling that someone was watching her slid down her spine.

Slowly, she turned toward the windows. Short shrubs lined the lower two feet, and the branches of a cedar tree danced in the breeze as clouds drifted across the moon.

It took a moment for her eyes to adjust. She could see no one, but the feeling of being watched grew.

"Everly, hurry up. We need to leave now."

Her daughter stood in the doorway with Dexter. "I'm ready."

But when Josie went to the front entryway to leave, she saw the silhouette of a man through the small pane on the door. He moved to the back of her Bronco, where the security light did not reach. Her hand shot out, and she whispered, "Go out the back door."

Everly's eyes grew large, but she hurried through the dark house to the back, evidently feeling the urgency.

"Leave your bag here." They dropped their stuff on the floor at the same time and all three of them fled the cabin to the backyard.

As soon as they moved under the covering of a huge pecan tree, Everly whispered, "Is the man here again?"

"Yes, honey, and it's important he doesn't hear us. Try to keep Dexter quiet."

Everly nodded. "Okay."

After they'd gone to the edge of the yard, about twenty yards from the home, Josie stopped. "Let's stay here and see if the man leaves. Be ready to move quickly."

Again, she nodded.

Poor thing. Josie hated scaring her, but it would do no good to go traipsing about in the woods. They wouldn't know if the gunman left the cabin, had someone pick him up or if he was following them. If it weren't for having Everly with her, Josie would confront the man. There was no way she could put her daughter's life at risk.

Her mind went back to the stranger who'd helped them. Surely it wasn't a coincidence. He knew they were headed back to the cabin, and the gunman was waiting for them. Why didn't the man give his name?

Dexter's ear went up as he stared toward the cabin.

The man stood at the back door, which meant he'd been inside and must now realize they'd spotted him.

Josie pulled Everly closer as she bent down. "Shh. Let's move back."

"That's him."

She gave her shoulder a squeeze and stepped deeper into the shadows. A narrow trail cut across the yard to a gate that led to the woods, but Josie kept to the left of it, afraid if the man ran after them, he'd stick to the path.

She patted her leg to draw Dexter's attention. Too late. The dog gave three quick barks.

"No, Dex." Everly's face lit up in alarm.

"Let's go!" Josie whisper-yelled. They took off

through the trees behind the shed and down the fence row.

A bullet whizzed past her ear, followed by the resounding pop. "Stay down." She returned fire, two shots with her Sig. As they weaved through the trees, Josie hoped to deter the gunman, but another shot blasted.

Wood splintered above them and a heavy limb from the pecan tree fell, hitting her on the top of the head. Pain radiated throughout her body as she hit the ground.

"Mom!"

"I'm okay." Josie struggled to stand, but not before Dexter licked her on the cheek. "We've got to keep moving."

"This way." Everly zigzagged through the trees.

But Josie's world spun out of control and lights danced before her, making it difficult to stay on her feet. She turned one last time and fired another shot toward the cabin. Hopefully, the gunman would keep his distance.

As the trees blended into the sky, the moon bounced up and down in a blur. Her head swirled, but she kept following Everly and Dexter. If they could just find a good hiding place.

"Come on. This way." Everly held back a bush branch so that Josie could get by. "You don't look good."

Josie would've laughed if it wasn't for her head

throbbing. She didn't ask where they were going because it didn't matter as long as it bought her time to get her bearings. They came to a clearing, and she recognized this was where she'd found Everly earlier. Her head continued to swim. "Stop. I need to rest."

"I'll go get help."

"No. We stick together." Josie drew a deep breath. The spinning slowed, but she didn't think it'd take much activity to grow worse again.

A twig snapped from somewhere close by. Both of them looked to the south from where the sound came. Dexter raised his hackles.

"Mom, did you hear that? It's either the man or the bear."

"Don't worry. I'll protect you." But could she keep her word? She had no choice but to get going. Her dizziness had only slightly lessened. "Let's move again."

A deep growl came from the west, sending chills down her spine. She hadn't believed there was a bear, but that certainly sounded like one. Seconds later, an engine rumbled from behind them to the south where the gunman would've been.

With danger coming for them from two directions, Josie picked up the pace to a run.

Everly said in a panicked voice, "Let me get help. I can do it faster without you."

Her words wreaked havoc on Josie's mind.

"From who? Not that stranger. He may be working with the gunman. You can't run off. It's too dangerous."

"Dane helped us. He told me his place was that way. Since he heard me screaming, he can't be far away."

Had the man told Josie his name? No, she didn't think so. He'd refused. There was only one person she knew who went by the name Dane.

Dane Haggerty.

Josie asked, "How do you know his name?"

"He told me when he was trying to get me to come out of the log."

No. Surely not. She would've recognized him. But his face was covered by a bushy beard, and he'd worn a cap low on his head. She could kick herself. He had never looked at her directly after he'd met her in the woods. Which meant he'd recognized her. *That low-down, good-for-nothing Haggerty boy.* Her grandfather's words played through her mind like it was yesterday.

Her cheeks burned with heat as they hiked through the wilderness. She'd turned Dane in once to the police for stealing a car their senior year in high school. And she'd seen the news that he was a suspect in a murder case. If there was any other option for protection, she'd choose it.

However, she had little choice but to seek refuge from a fugitive.

* * *

Dane took long strides toward his hideout. Unknown to Josie, he'd followed the duo at a distance to the cabin to make certain they arrived safely. At first, he couldn't help but think the gunman may've been a bounty hunter hoping to bring him in.

But now he was ninety percent certain the man had targeted Josie and her daughter if Everly had truly witnessed her father's murder. He kept a constant watch for a sign of the man. He had started to keep an eye on the cabin until Josie left, but then he got to thinking about his hideout. If it were a bounty hunter, he might be in search of his place right now.

He pulled his burner cell phone out of his pocket, but there was no signal. Hopefully, reception would improve when he got back to his place.

Maybe he should find a new hideout. Either way, Dane needed transportation, and his old truck was back at the barn he used for cover. He hurried through the trees toward his shelter while keeping a lookout for the bear.

Frustration bit at him. His life had been on a solid trajectory for several years, giving him confidence that staying on the straight and narrow had served him well. After working in the construction business for seven years, he finally took a leap of faith and started North Texas Custom

Builders with his good friend, Harlan Schmidt. The business had its bumps in the road, but nothing that hard work and careful planning hadn't solved. Then, several months ago, Child Protective Services took his younger sister away from his mom and put Violet into foster care for neglect. It's not that he doubted his mom had not taken good care of his sister—his mom had always battled problems from drinking to putting food on the table. But he could only imagine how it felt to be forced to live with strangers—following new family rules and maybe going to a new school. Everything Violet had ever known ripped from underneath her. That in itself could create a whole list of new problems, even if the foster family were decent and kind people. Dane hoped to gain custody of his younger sister and filed with the court.

Yes, things had not been seamless, but his life derailed four months ago when he walked in to find Harlan lying on the floor in Dane's office with his granddaddy's antique hay hook embedded in his back. Uncertain if Harlan was breathing, he tried to remove the hook from his back so he could roll him over. But it was no use. Someone must've called the police because a cruiser pulled into the drive and Dane took off out the back.

He probably shouldn't have run, but the timing had been too perfect, and Dane had been on the losing side of the law before. Within hours, a warrant had been issued for his arrest, and he'd been running ever since. He planned to turn himself in once he found evidence to clear his name.

Even though he hadn't seen Josie in years, he'd heard she worked with the sheriff's department as an investigator for a while. Was she being near him just a coincidence? He doubted it. Maybe she was a bounty hunter.

He rubbed his hands through his hair. Not only was he not making good progress figuring out who murdered Harlan because it was too risky to return to his house or the office to search for evidence, but now he had to wonder if his hideout was compromised. He couldn't hide out forever, but he'd hoped to be closer to figuring out who framed him.

Harlan had believed money was missing from North Texas Custom Builders, and there had to be a paper trail. Making matters worse was the fact that money had shown up in his own account that Dane hadn't deposited himself.

It would make it easier if Dane had family or someone in law enforcement who was looking to clear his name, but his family was the last place he could turn. A glance to his Bible reminded him of the verse in Ecclesiastes he'd read earlier in the day. *Two are better than one; because they have a good reward for their labour.*

Harlan had been his closest friend and had introduced him to God. Maybe if Dane had been a better friend to others, he might have someone else to turn to.

He'd listened to scanners and read the news daily to catch updates about the murder case, but all information had dropped to virtually nothing after the first two weeks. The past four months had been the longest of his life.

Darkness shrouded the old wooden barn. Tree limbs blew in the breeze and crickets chirped. Stopping at the edge of the woods, he watched his hideout for several minutes. No strange sounds or movements could be detected. Slowly, he stepped through the weeds, sticking close to the protection of the trees. He walked around the perimeter and then moved in.

A minute later, he unlocked the chain on the barn's double doors and put his hand on the thick handle to open it when he heard a voice. He froze.

There it was again.

Dropping the chain, he stepped outside into the shadows.

A slight figure ran toward him, and a dog barked. As the girl grew closer, her features became clear.

Panting for breath, Everly said, "The man came back. Mom… Mom needs help."

His chest tightened. "Show me." He headed in the direction, but someone came out of the darkness.

"It's me." Josie's voice sounded tired, and maybe a tad angry. "Don't shoot."

He never should've left them alone. He hurried her way, but when he got close, her hand shot in the air.

"Dane Haggerty, if you'll help us get away, I promise I won't turn you in to authorities until I get back to Liberty."

All air left his lungs as his shoulders slumped. All the trying to live right, to change his life for good, had brought him back full circle. His fate lay in Josie Hunt's hands. He was certain he didn't like that at all.

THREE

Josie's head throbbed as she rubbed her forehead, but they didn't have time to stand around.

Dane stepped beside her. "Let me see that." He gently removed her hand. "Ouch."

She instinctively pulled away from his touch. "Our guy fired at us and caused a heavy limb to fall on me. I'm fine."

Everly stepped close. "My daddy's killer was at our cabin, and we came looking for you."

Dane glanced from Everly to Josie. "Did he see where you went?"

"No, but I know which way he went. We heard something crashing in the woods and then an engine. He has some kind of vehicle."

"We need to get you to a hospital and away from here. Come on."

When Josie tried to walk, her knees wobbled, causing her to stumble into him.

"There's no time for this." Dane scooped her into his arms and headed in the direction they'd been traveling.

"Wait. This isn't necessary. The hit on the head made me a little loopy, but I'm feeling better."

His dark eyes stared down at her. "We have no time. I don't want to be caught in the open."

She was used to doing things herself, but even as the thought came to her, her head swam, dizziness causing her to close her eyes and lean against the strong shoulder. Her stomach didn't feel so good. Nausea was a sign of a concussion. Maybe he was right.

Even as she kept her eyes closed while trying to stop the swirling, she listened to the sound of his footsteps. A minute later, he paused, and she opened her eyes.

He swung a wooden door wide and carried her into a large building—a barn. The constant moving up and down made it difficult to concentrate on what she was seeing. He opened another door and then put her down on a leather couch.

"Where is Everly?"

"I'm right here." Her daughter moved beside her.

Josie squinted. "Is this a camper?"

"Yes."

She went to sit up but grabbed her head in pain. "I need to call my boss."

"Maybe later."

"No. We have people on my team and in the sheriff's department who can help. Law officers need to arrest the shooter before he hurts anyone else. And if he is the one who killed Pierce, he needs to be off the streets."

Dane frowned. "We're out of Jarvis County's jurisdiction."

"There's someone out there with a gun who's targeting us." Even though Everly knew they were in danger, Josie thought it best not to use the phrase "he's trying to kill us." The girl was scared enough already. "I know you're running from the law, but we must get out of here."

He frowned. "Did you get a better look at him this time? Did you recognize him?"

She shook her head and instantly regretted it. "I'm certain he was watching while we were packing in the cabin. I glanced out the door before opening it and saw him standing beside my Bronco with the rifle, like he was waiting for us. We left our things and hurried out the back door." Maybe if she'd been by herself, she could've challenged him since she was armed, but all she could think of was getting Everly away from this guy. "It was too dark to see his features, but he was tall and slim."

"I'm assuming the guy followed you."

"Probably. We heard something moving in the trees, and I think your bear friend was out there, too."

Quickly, he turned to a kitchen cabinet. "I have ibuprofen if you need it."

"I'd appreciate that. I'll take one. Do you have a vehicle?"

She sat against the cushions, pushing aside the headache. After she took the medicine, she glanced around at the granite countertops, nice stainless-steel refrigerator, and a genuine wood floor. Everything looked top of the line. It hadn't escaped her attention that he didn't argue about being a fugitive. "This is a nice camper. Yours?"

Dexter whimpered and came over to the couch, looking at Josie with his tail wagging.

"I'm all right, Dex." She patted his head, then turned her gaze back to Dane. "Is this RV in a barn, or did I imagine that?"

"It's a barn. Helps keep the energy costs down."

"Yeah." She laughed. "And keeps it hidden from those nearby. Great hideout." The sarcasm wasn't necessary, but she tended to lean on it when she was nervous.

His gaze met hers, but he didn't say a word.

Her eyes squinted. "Do you have a phone I can borrow? Earlier, you said you'd call the sheriff's department. Did you do that?"

"I tried. Here you go." He pulled a cell phone from his pocket and held it out to her. "This place is hard to find, but if you found it, someone else can, too. I need to make certain the gunman didn't follow you." Before she had time to react, he turned and stepped out of the camper.

Oh no, you don't. She struggled to her feet and waited several seconds to get her bearings before moving toward the door. Everly and Dexter followed her.

The barn was tall and open, but the camper took up much of the space. She saw Dane walk between the home and a motorcycle that was propped against the wall to the back door. A rusty pickup truck that was parked inside looked to have seen better days. Probably didn't run.

Slowly, he pushed the door open and stepped outside.

They needed help, and fast. A glance at his cell phone showed two bars, and she punched 9-1-1.

Where did he go? She stepped toward the door he'd exited.

The dispatcher answered, "9-1-1. What is your emergency?"

"My name is Josie Hunt, a man shot at me and my daughter..."

Something clanked from outside. The door swung open, and Dane hurried inside with a gun in his hand when a gunshot blasted.

The cell phone went flying out of her hand and landed on the floor in pieces. More bullets sprayed the doorframe, sending wood splinters into the air.

Everly squealed and moved behind Josie.

Dexter sprinted underneath the pickup and launched into a barking tirade.

"Our shooter is back. Get in my truck. Now." He hurried to the driver's side and put Everly in the middle as Josie ran to the passenger door. Dexter leaped onto the floorboard before climbing onto Josie's lap. "Put your heads down. Hang on."

More gunfire from outside.

When he turned the key, his old Ford roared to life, and he stomped on the gas.

One of the big double doors swung wide, and the gunman stepped into the opening, taking aim. This guy looked heavier than the one she'd seen at the cabin.

Dane's truck hesitated, spinning in loose hay. They gained traction, shot forward and blasted through the doors.

The gunman leaped out of the way barely in time.

One of the barn's doors ripped from its hinges and landed on the hood before sliding off.

The man shot several more times, once hitting Dane's side window.

"Is this guy trying to kill all of us?" Josie yelled over the roaring engine.

"I don't know. I can ask him later."

As he flew down the grassy drive, headlights came from in front of them.

"Dane! Watch out!"

He jerked the wheel to the left and into a barb-wire fence to avoid hitting the other vehicle. T-posts bent under the impact and dented the front of his bumper. After half the fence was gone, he pulled the wheel back to the right, ran over brush and kept going.

Josie looked over the seat. Headlights from a pickup bounced through the pasture, making a wide circle. "He's turning around."

"There's two of them."

She glanced again. Sure enough, another set of headlights, but narrower, flew out from behind his barn.

"One looks to be a four-wheeler or some kind of ATV." At the end of the grass drive, he turned left onto the rock road without slowing down.

A dust cloud appeared in the reflection from the brake lights. On the left, she saw the ATV tearing through the pasture parallel to them.

Everly covered her ears and bent forward with her head lowered. Dexter had already crawled back to the floorboard, evidently not liking the bumpy ride.

Josie called out, "Do you know where you're going?"

"I've been this way several times. Right now, I'm just trying to get away."

She checked the twenty-round magazine on her Sig and then slid it back into her pocket but didn't fasten it shut. Her two extra magazines were locked in a case in the back of the Bronco. Tension racked her body as they came to a sharp curve. Dane hit his brakes as he slid through the turn. Centripetal force tugged his tires into the ditch before they got back to the middle of the road. She held onto the door handle with one hand while the other squeezed the back of Everly's shirt, trying to keep her upright.

The road came to another *T*. When he hesitated, Josie asked, "Are you familiar with this area?"

"I don't recognize this road. Did you call the sheriff?"

She yelled. "I tried, but a bullet hit your phone, destroying it. Sorry."

"This is not good."

As they neared a wooden bridge, a large grove of trees appeared to the left. Just as he was in the middle of the dilapidated passage, the ATV shot out from the brush, headlights blaring through the driver's side window.

"Watch out." Josie looked back over her shoulder as the headlights shone in the back window. "Everly, I want you to stay down. Okay?"

"Okay." The girl frowned and sank lower into the seat.

"I'm going to get him to back off." Josie rolled down the passenger side window and climbed into the opening and sat on the door frame. She aimed her Sig and fired three shots.

Dane's truck hit a pothole, sending it jolting.

"Whoa." Her heart leaped, and her free hand

grabbed the interior of the cab, regaining her balance.

The driver swerved and backed off.

She plopped back into her seat. "That should get him to keep his distance."

Dane glanced her way. "I thought you were an investigator, not a deputy. I'm assuming you worked in the field and did more than search documents on a computer from the office when you were employed at the sheriff's department."

Her gaze connected with his. "You could say that."

Headlights came from in front of him. She realized the driver must know these back roads as well as Dane. "Here we go again. Hang on."

A sour taste bubbled up in her throat as she braced for more danger, and she prayed they got out of this alive.

Dane had to get off the road before the two men sandwiched them in. If he was alone, maybe he could take the chance. But not with Josie and Everly with him.

A rocky driveway appeared up ahead. John-songrass grew around a large metal sign, making it impossible to read. He figured it'd be best to take his chances than to hit the other truck. He whipped into the driveway. Not knowing what kind of place this was, he slowed down a tad.

Headlights shone in his rearview mirror, and

another set came from the trees. He had to lose these guys.

After a mile or so, they topped out on a large hill. A giant sand hole spread out in front of them. Dane swerved right to keep on the rim that was covered with small trees.

Josie leaned over to peer out his side of the window. "That looks like some kind of quarry."

"Yeah, one that hasn't been used in years." His truck bounced with the rugged terrain. Narrow gullies created by rainwater streaked across the rim.

Lights again shone on his back window. "They're gaining on us."

He pressed the gas pedal, but the engine roared, and the truck slowed. "This can't be happening."

"What's wrong?"

"I think my transmission is out." He shifted the gear into neutral and then back to drive again, but the truck rolled to a stop.

"Dane, we need to move."

"I'm trying." He slammed it into Park before shifting into Drive, but it was no use. As the gunmen bore down on them, he rammed the gear into Reverse. The transmission popped, and the truck jumped. As shots sprayed the hood, he spun the truck around and took off, going backward.

"Whoa!" Everly yelled as she fell sideways. She climbed into the seat.

Josie joined in. "Oh... Dane!"

He dodged trees and worked to keep the tires on the rim of the giant man-made hole, avoiding cave-ins on the edge.

Josie leaned forward and dug her fingers into the dash.

The quarry took in about ten acres with deep, steep sides. If he were to go over the edge, the truck would roll. The other vehicle, a black Dodge, took off around the other side, its lights bouncing with the movement. With only his backup lights, he could barely see where he was going. Red reflected on the tree trunks, barely giving him time to react. Like a ball in a pinball game, he weaved in and out of the brush.

The pickup flew up on them, being able to go faster forward. Headlights blinded him, making him glance away.

He warned, "Hang on."

The Dodge slammed into his front bumper, sending them fishtailing toward the outside of the rim into the trees. Everly planted her feet against the dash, just as they were hit again. "Ow." She removed her feet and returned to the floorboard beside Dexter.

Branches scraped the side of his truck. Their bumpers stayed locked as the other truck pushed them faster.

"That's enough." Josie fired two quick shots out the window.

The truck kept coming but gave them distance.

She looked back in the other direction. "The ATV is headed this way."

"Great. I really don't want to hit the guy."

Her hand touched his arm. "Try not to do that." She glanced at Everly as she lay with her head in Josie's lap.

"I understand." As his truck continued to bounce and run along the overgrowth, he looked for a way out. In less than twenty seconds, the ATV would come up behind him. While trying to keep his truck from going over the rim's edge, he searched for an escape.

Suddenly, his headlights flashed on a road that snaked down into the hole used by the haul trucks. In his mirror, the ATV swung wide, getting ready to force him into the pit. He had to take this opportunity. "Hang on."

Everly squealed as he jerked the wheel to the right, whipping the truck toward the rim in a tight circle until he was hightailing it back toward the ramp.

Brake lights flashed from the ATV before it slammed into a tree. The other truck continued coming his way.

Keeping the accelerator pressed, he descended the ramp, spiraling downward.

"I hope you know what you're doing!" Josie held on to Everly and the dashboard.

Parts of the ramp were washed away, and he gritted his teeth as they hit each crevice. He could only see the quarry in bits and pieces as he made his way down the incline, but it looked to have water in the bottom. There was no way to tell how deep it was. If he made it to the base, then what?

They'd be trapped.

He'd known that was a possibility when he'd chosen this route, but his goal was to ensnare their pursuers here and then hightail it out, a risky tactic, but he'd been in dicey situations before.

On the other side of the pit, the truck raced down the road. With only Reverse, there was no way to outrun these guys. Once they got near the bottom, the gunmen could easily pick them off.

"What's the plan? Do we need to get out and run for it?"

"We don't know how much ammunition they have. I only have about twenty more cartridges besides what's in my gun."

"I'm a skilled marksman, but I'd hate to get shot down with no help for miles."

It'd been years since he'd participated in stunts of jumping his motorcycle and leaping ravines in his old Mustang. He'd even bungee jumped strapped to a couch from a railroad overpass. He wasn't that guy anymore and had spent years trying to redeem himself and prove he could be a businessman and an asset to the community.

Not that it had stopped him from being framed for murder.

But he'd never had an innocent woman and child with him. He glanced at her. "Do you trust me?"

"Not really." She looked at him with scrutiny. "But do I have a choice?"

Ouch. He had to admit she had little alternative. "I'll get us out of here. Make certain your daughter's seatbelt is snug. It tends to loosen easily." He patted the seat. "Just try to keep your head low."

Josie nodded and then did as he asked.

He didn't know if he could get out of this pit, but he wasn't ready to give up. Still going in Reverse, he turned the truck off the road and straight up the pit. As no one had excavated the quarry in years, the sand was packed, and the thick vegetation should give him traction. It was crucial he back straight up and not sideways, or else they would roll.

His passengers were silent as the engine revved, plowing up the sandy terrain.

He glanced at Josie and noticed her eyes were closed. Whether scared or praying, he didn't know.

The back end slid to the right, where the ground broke off in a serious crevice. He fought to keep the momentum. His tires slid, but he kept the gas down and slowly his old truck slithered toward the top of the hill.

Below them, the gunman's truck slid sideways,

the driver foolishly jerking the wheel to the right, which was the wrong move. The truck careened down the pit and crashed into a bottomless ravine. Seconds later, steam floated from under the hood.

"Let's go," Josie shouted.

Dane made it to the rim and took off toward the exit, trying not to jolt his passengers. But it was no use. The road was simply too rough. All was quiet in the cab as they made it back to the road, and then he maneuvered through the countryside going backwards. He hoped the transmission didn't totally go out.

A loud sigh came from his passenger once they had traveled several miles away from the quarry. "I have to admit. Your driving abilities are just as good as they were in high school."

He didn't look her way. "Thanks. I think."

When they got to safety, *if* they made it safety, did he escort her to the sheriff's department? Even as the thought crossed his mind, his stomach knotted. Could he give up Violet so easily?

Suddenly, the engine grew loud, and the truck rolled to a stop. He and Josie exchanged glances. He put it in and out of gear several times, but the vehicle didn't move. "Looks like this is as far as it goes."

Josie gazed out her window. "At least we're miles from the quarry and the gunmen."

"True."

As they got out on the passenger side in the tall grass, Everly lifted her shoe. "Oh."

"What's wrong?" Josie asked as she knelt beside her and felt her foot. When her hands touched the ankle, Everly grimaced.

Dane came around their side of the truck.

Dexter sniffed the girl's foot like he understood it bothered her. Josie stared at her daughter. "Can you walk on it?"

Everly took a few steps, but then limped.

"Come on. I've got you." Dane scooped her into his arms.

"I can carry my own daughter."

"I realize that. I'll give you a turn when I get tired. Deal?"

A slight smile tugged at her lips. "Thanks, Dane."

Her tiny gesture shed a sliver of light into a dark situation. "Let's stay close to the road until daylight. If the guys return, we should see their headlights in plenty of time to get out of sight."

Everly laid her head against his shoulder, and almost immediately, her eyes closed.

They walked for several minutes, and he noted Josie's frown only deepened. "Are you okay? Is your head still hurting?"

"I have a slight headache, but it's not as strong. The good news is I'm no longer dizzy."

"That's good." He hated seeing her this way. "I know my truck is broken down, and we're miles from your vehicle, but if it's any consolation, I plan to see you back to safety."

Her gaze cut to him like she was insinuating he didn't have a clue.

"What?"

"Don't you get it? These guys are serious about doing what is necessary to stop Everly from identifying her father's murderer. And now we've been added to the equation. That means killing all three of us."

FOUR

As the three of them hiked through the pasture under the light of the moon, Josie had time to ponder their situation. The main concern was to get to her Bronco so they could contact the sheriff of McCade County or find a phone to call for assistance.

"What can I do to help?" Dane asked.

"I don't know. Nothing." Irritation crept into her tone. She kept her gaze on where she was going instead of looking at him. She had been too busy with her daughter to think about him, but she couldn't help being annoyed that he had stolen that car, thus rupturing their friendship years ago. He'd shattered her trust—something she didn't give easily. Even though Dane had always been carefree and rambunctious, she never thought he'd break the law. After he was sent off to juvenile detention to finish out his senior year, she had mostly stayed to herself. Selena and Bridgett had been her friends, but once they began dating guys, it was like she was the third wheel.

Spending time with her granddad was a gift—no matter how eccentric, and even sometimes embarrassing, she found him when she young. His hobby of making music with spoons had been exciting and curious to some, but for a teenager who'd moved to a new school, it'd brought unwanted attention when he performed at local events. A few times a week, he'd meet his friends and practice, and occasionally they'd play at festivals or break out the spoons after a meal at a local diner. It was one thing she and Dane had in common—they were two of a few teens who didn't have a parent at home. She lived with a grandparent, and he lived in different places—sometimes with a neighbor and other times with his grandmother.

"I didn't do it."

"Do what?"

"You're thinking about me stealing Principal Scruggs's Mustang. I didn't knowingly steal it. Keaton Stebbins gave me the keys and told me to take *his* car for a spin. Looking back, it wasn't too bright of me, but I believed him and was excited to show off my driving skills."

She sighed and shook her head. They'd had this short and to-the-point discussion eleven years ago in high school. "I'm not going to argue because I saw you, Dane. I wished I hadn't, but I did. The red Mustang pulled out of Principal Scruggs's driveway, and you were the one to get out of the driver's seat at Talley Field. Everyone knew the Mustang belonged to Scruggs."

"Not me." He shook his head. "I was a dumb kid, trying to get attention. But I was no thief. Like I said, Keaton gave me the keys. I assumed that was *his* house and *his* car. I didn't ask questions. I was just glad to be included."

Josie refused to argue with him. She knew what she saw, even though it brought her no pleasure. Did he really expect her to believe he didn't know the muscle car belonged to the principal? Keaton Stebbins's dad was the county district attorney. From what Josie knew of Keaton, he was a good kid. Dane had disappointed her more than she let anyone know. She had needed him back then. Before her family had perished in the fire and Josie had been the sole survivor, she'd been confident and had plenty of friends. Then in one moment, everything changed.

"I'm not my dad."

Not in everything, no. "I never said you were."

He squinted his eyes at her, indicating he knew what she thought. "You want to tell me about Everly's dad?"

His change of subject was a relief. "I don't know what there is to tell. He was a great man—a caring dad and a competent investigator."

He nodded. "So, he was an investigator. That's how you met him."

"Yeah. I got into law enforcement with the encouragement of my granddad, a family tradition type of thing, but you knew my plans. We talked about our futures enough times." Not only had her granddad been a small-town police officer, but he also had a couple of retired friends from the department who had invited her to spend time with their families. To this day, Granddad spent time with two of his retired police buddies playing spoons and talking about the old days. "Even though Pierce didn't work for the sheriff's department, occasionally we'd talk on the phone or see each other in the same circles."

She glanced at Dane. Everly's head was snuggled into his neck, her long braids dangling down to his chest, and she was still fast asleep. Poor thing. She was sure to be missing her dad, which probably made her instant attachment to Dane unavoidable.

"How long were you two married?"

She stopped in her tracks. "What? We weren't married."

"Oh. Sorry." He shrugged. "I just assumed…"

If the situation weren't so serious, she might've laughed. "He wasn't my boyfriend either."

Confusion etched across his brow.

"His wife died six years ago, and upon his death, Everly was left alone with no family who wanted to take in an eight-year-old. I adopted her."

"I didn't know."

Was that relief in his expression? She shook her head, and a smile crept up.

Dane threw his free hand in the air defensively. "Being shot at hasn't exactly given us time to talk. I guess you've never been married?"

"No. And you?"

He shook his head. "Too busy trying to build the business with Harlan. I've gone out on a few dates."

She almost laughed out loud. Even though she hadn't seen Dane in years, in a graduating class of forty-one, everyone tended to keep up with one another. One of her friends, Tara, had told her she'd heard Dane had moved about thirty minutes west of Liberty and was working in construction. Then a couple of years ago, Susan told her Dane had gone into business for himself, and she saw him driving a black sports car with a pretty blonde in the passenger seat. Susan laughed and made a crack wondering if he'd stolen the car.

Being annoyed, Josie had quickly cut Susan's conversation short. She didn't know if it was the callous joke or that Dane was with a girl, but she had no desire to talk anymore.

Josie had dated a couple of guys, but nothing serious. She didn't want to discuss her personal life with Dane or anyone. Personal life. Ha. As if she had one. The last few years, her energy and time had been taken up with her private investigation company and volunteering with the Bring the Children Home Project. There were times she longed to have someone besides her grandfather to share good news with—such as when a missing child was reunited with their family. Or like last year when she was shot under the ribcage while helping Chandler Murphy, the K-9 handler for the team, work a case to find a missing boy. It would've been nice to have someone at her side during her hospital stay and recovery. But at what cost? How would she deal with it if she lost someone else? She didn't know if she could survive that kind of loss again.

One thing was certain, she didn't need to be distracted with Dane. Her daughter had to be her top priority. "I'll take Everly now."

Dane started to tell her he could handle carrying the girl, especially since Everly might be too heavy and awkward for Josie to carry. He could see that Josie had made up her mind, so he handed her daughter over.

Once Josie positioned her against her chest, and her arms were securely wrapped around the girl, they took off again.

He shouldn't have cared that Josie wasn't married, but he was glad. Even though their relationship had ended terribly, he had thought of her often and occasionally looked her up on social media. It had been a year or more since he'd searched. That was why he'd been so surprised to realize she had a daughter. He couldn't figure out how he had missed that when most people posted news of their kids all the time. Now it made sense.

Back in high school, she had been the one person who seemed to *get* him. He told himself she was too good for him. Since they'd lived on the same road, they had gotten to know each other. One day his car—his grandmother's vehicle that he drove—broke down some five miles from his house, and he started walking. Josie came along and gave him a ride the rest of the way home. Since neither had a vehicle of their own but used their grandparents', they began to share rides and soon talked for hours like best friends. The summer between his junior and senior year, they'd finally begun to date.

Going out with Josie had been the first sign of hope in his life, a sign that made him believe he didn't have to turn out like his family. He'd heard the whispers, and sometimes experienced downright animosity because of his family. It was no secret to the community his dad, Tyrus, had done time in prison for theft. The theft had been personal to many in the community. He loved not only to steal from neighbors when they went on vacation or were at work, but also to nab packages that were delivered to businesses and homes. Many times, Dane thought how much his dad would've loved the apps nowadays that show where the delivery trucks were making stops.

But it was when his dad turned to robbing banks that the authorities really took notice. If he had just robbed the one bank, he may've never been caught. But it was dad's third time that did him in. There was an off-duty police officer in the lobby who took him down.

His dad caught pneumonia while in prison and died after only serving two years.

His older brother, Randy, had been sent to an alternative school for threatening a teacher with a knife. Before Josie, Dane had tried to do anything for attention—most of the time it leaned toward the dangerous side. Like riding his motorcycle recklessly and trying stunts. It had worked, too. Kids took notice of him and so did the adults.

"Oh." Josie tripped over something, almost causing her to fall with Everly.

He stepped forward to prepare to catch her. "Are you all right?"

"I'm fine. I stepped in a hole."

The girl wiggled in Josie's arms and opened her eyes, before falling back asleep.

"If you need me to take another turn, I don't mind." But as he figured, she shook her head, not taking him up on his offer.

After a few minutes he asked, "What was in the police report from when Everly's dad died?"

"I don't think there was a police report, but only the autopsy. I didn't realize anything at the time was suspect. I received a copy of the official documents when I adopted her, but with Pierce's house being in probate, the estate needed to be cleaned out, so I never saw the need to dig further, and I haven't gone back over everything."

"Totally understandable. Sounds like the police didn't either."

"I should've gone through everything by now. It's my job to perform mundane activities like sifting through paperwork. My daughter had been living with this burden for months…"

"Josie, you can't beat yourself up over this. There was no way you could know." She didn't respond but kept trekking across the pasture. He understood wanting to blame oneself for not noticing something like that, but it could only prove a distraction to her ability to keep Everly safe now.

Dane mulled over the situation, and ways to make it easier on them kept returning to his mind. "I'd like to run ahead and retrieve your Bronco to come back and pick you two up, so you don't have to walk. Or I could get my motorcycle and ride it to get your vehicle. Would you be comfortable with that if we find a place for you to hide?"

She shook her head. "That thought crossed my

mind, too. But I think we'd be safer sticking together. Two guns are better than one should the two men find us. Even if you aren't trained."

Dane didn't particularly like being reminded he wasn't trained to use a gun. He'd hunted when he was younger and knew how to shoot. Evening the score should another shoot-out happen had occurred to him, too. "I can protect us if need be."

"It'd be helpful if we knew the men's identities."

Everly's head popped up. "Has my daddy's killer found us again?"

Josie exchanged glances with Dane as she patted Everly on the back. "No, baby. We were just talking."

They needed to be careful of what they discussed in front of the girl. No doubt she was scared enough. He couldn't imagine Violet being in this predicament.

"Honey, what happened to your dad?" Josie asked.

Brown eyes stared at Josie. "I don't want…"

"It's okay." Josie smiled. "No one's going to hurt me or you."

Dane's gut tightened at the heartbreaking concern that laced Josie's voice.

"My daddy and me were working in the backyard. He was using the weed trimmer, and I was putting away my toys. The man drove up, and Daddy started talking to him. I went inside to get us something to drink and use the bathroom. When I came out of the bathroom, I heard yelling and ran to the window. The man hit my dad in the face and then they started fighting. I yelled for them to stop. The man pulled a knife and tried to stab my dad. Daddy was too fast and dodged.

"I screamed. When Daddy looked at me, the man tackled him into the hot tub and held him under. When Daddy stopped kicking, the man saw me, and I ran out the front door and hid in my treehouse. Dexter had been barking and growling. I peeked through the window to see Dex bite the man's arm.

"And then a delivery truck pulled up. The man yelled at me that he would kill me like he did my dad if I told anyone. Then he ran into the woods."

"Oh, honey, I'm so sorry."

He wished Everly would've told Josie, but the killer had made certain she was too scared. Dane clenched his jaw. How could a man threaten the girl? "Do you know the man's name? Had you ever seen him before?"

Everly shook her head. "Never."

Josie glanced over her shoulder at Dane. "We need to let—" she cleared her throat "—let authorities know about this as soon as possible."

"No. No." Everly wiggled in her grasp. "He'll kill me."

Josie released a sigh as she clung to her daughter. "I'll protect you. Do you understand? As long as you're with me, nothing is going to happen to you."

A long hill appeared in front of them, and Dane held out his hands. "Can I have a turn?"

Creases lined Josie's forehead, but she handed over the girl.

As soon as Everly was in his arms, he asked, "How's that foot feeling?"

"It's hurts a little."

"Not too bad?"

"I can walk."

"How about you let me carry you for a while, at least as far as your mama did. You wouldn't want me to think your mama is stronger than me, would you?"

She giggled. "No."

Dexter trotted beside them, occasionally sniffing the ground and wandering in and out of the brush.

Josie whispered, "I'll be glad when I can call my boss and get some protection."

He would keep them safe. He'd be glad when Josie understood that. They had to be several miles from the cabin. He wasn't certain how far they would go, but they needed to keep heading south. He had stayed around the barn and had traveled into town a few times but hadn't gone in this direction much at all.

"I never thought I would say this, but I wish

there were more houses out this way. A farm—anything."

"I know what you mean."

The night sounds were mild with only a gentle breeze blowing the grass and an occasional bawl of a cow. Not even the chirp of crickets or croaking of frogs could be heard, so when a light hum sounded in the distance, he looked at Josie and said, "Let's move closer to the tree line."

"You think that's them?"

"I'd say so. Not much traffic this time of night out here."

Everly's eyes grew large. "They found us again?"

"Everything is going to be okay. You can count on it." He tapped her under the chin to show his confidence in his words.

Headlights suddenly appeared behind them.

Keeping one step ahead of these guys might be more complicated than initially thought. "It's time to run."

FIVE

They hurried across the open pasture, and the trees had to be a hundred yards away.

A cow bawled and then another. The Angus herd came into view as they topped the hill—their stocky black bodies barely detectable in the moonlight.

Josie looked over her shoulder as headlights bounced along the path. The bashed-up truck flew up the road. The guys should be coming up on their disabled truck. Sure enough, the men stopped. "They must know our vehicle broke down."

A few seconds later, the men took off again.

Lights shone in the pasture on the opposite side of the road and then swung back in their direction.

Dane yelled, "Get down."

She dropped to her stomach in the tall grass, Dane beside her. He put a protective arm around Everly. "Stay down, honey."

"Lie down, Dexter." The collie sprawled next

to Everly. Her daughter didn't say a word, but the fear on her face said enough.

A door slammed, and something crossed in front of the lights. The men were walking around. "Are they searching for beaten-down grass to determine which way we went?"

"Looks like it."

Suddenly, the man hurried back into the truck and gassed it toward them through the pasture. The urge to get up and run for the trees called her name, but then they'd give away their hiding place. Indecision plagued her. "You think we should run for it?"

"Wait." He held up a finger. "I doubt our tracks are that visible."

"But they may have nothing else to do but drive around. I can't just lie here and wait for them to find us. Everly, come with me but stay low." She got to her feet and took off when the headlights swung away from them. "Go."

Her daughter ran, but it was slow and with a limp. Dane scooped her up. They'd gone only about twenty yards when he again yelled, "Down."

They all dropped again. Josie watched the lights bounce across the terraces in the pasture. *Dear God, help us know what to do. I don't want to get in a shoot-out.*

The cows continued to bawl and suddenly an idea crossed her mind. She'd probably watched too many Westerns, but people were always using a stampede in the movies. That probably wasn't a good idea unless the men were on foot. As soon as the truck turned in a parallel direction, she said, "Come on. And don't stop."

They ran across the open field, Josie moving fast. Even while carrying Everly, Dane remained close to her side. Dexter stayed beside them. Only fifty more yards until they would be under the protection of the trees, and the area illuminated around them.

The engine revved as it came across the open place, and the cattle watched. A few of the calves trotted to get beside their mothers.

A gunshot went off.

They weren't going to make it. Her boot stepped into a hole, and she almost went down. As she regained her footing another shot went off.

She drew her gun. "Go. Get to the trees."

But instead of doing as she said, Dane put Everly on the ground. He removed his gun from his waistband. "I've got this. Hurry. Protect the girl."

Josie wanted to argue, but he was right. She picked Everly up and sprinted as fast as she could for the woods with Dexter.

"I can walk." Everly squirmed in her grasp.

"Not yet."

Dane fired his Glock, and then more shots

were returned at them. One whizzed past Josie's head, and she ducked as if it would help.

There was more bawling from the cattle, and then they were running. The herd turned straight at them with several cows leading the pack, jumping over brush and dodging others. The stampede had started. There was nowhere to go. Not knowing what else to do, she waved her free arm at the cows and yelled, "Yaw! Get back!"

The herd split, and she was able to make for the trees. She put Everly down behind a large pecan tree. "Stay behind the trunk with Dexter. I don't want you getting hit by a stray bullet."

"Okay. Be careful."

She made eye contact and gave her daughter a reassuring smile. "I will."

When she turned around, the truck was still heading toward them, but Dane was nowhere in sight. The sound of gunfire had dissipated among the running cattle. Her heart sped up as she looked around. The cows were still on the move, but she could barely see them on the far side of the pasture.

A few washes cut across the land and the truck bounced up and down as it made tracks toward them.

"Where's Dane?" Everly asked.

"I don't know, but he knows how to stay out of trouble." Ever since the day she'd met him, he'd been good at getting out of messes, even dangerous ones. She hoped he did this time as well. "We need to keep moving."

But as they headed deeper into the woods, she wondered what had happened to him. Had he taken off to escape and wasn't coming back? Or had he been trampled by the cattle?

There was no benefit to fretting about her ex-boyfriend. Her focus needed to be on getting Everly to safety and figuring out how she was going to get to her vehicle.

Before the men found them again.

Dane lay in the tall grass, the back of his leg throbbing with pain. A cow had rushed toward him. He'd tried to move but wasn't quick enough. He was knocked to the ground and then another cow tried to leap him, but her back leg came down on his hamstring.

He'd seen Josie and Everly make it into the thicket. He was glad they kept going and didn't wait for him. The men were almost to the trees. Their window was down, and their hollering at each other was easy to hear. "In there. She disappeared into the woods."

Oh no, you don't. He aimed his Glock and waited for them to draw closer. *Closer. Closer.* When they were thirty yards in front of him, he shot. Sparks from the bullet hit the side of the cab.

One of the men yelled something and returned fire, but his aim was off since they didn't know his location. He waited for the vehicle to pass. Josie couldn't be seen, but the truck made several passes. Finally, the driver stopped, and his passenger got out and headed into the woods. The truck proceeded along the tree line in the direction of the cabin.

Dane's chest tightened. He had hoped the men wouldn't separate. Once the truck had gone farther away, he climbed to his feet and made his way toward the trees. The back of his leg cramped but he was determined not to let it slow him down. Following at a distance, he stayed to the edge of the tree line while being on the lookout for Josie.

There was no noise, which concerned him. After all this time, he still couldn't believe he was helping Josie Hunt. He'd had a crush on her in high school, but like many others, it took a while for her to know he existed. Once they began to talk, they'd become friends almost instantly. He'd felt betrayed when she told the police he was the one responsible for the theft. And if he was totally honest, deeply hurt. She had acted like he'd let her down. Well, he wouldn't disappoint her this time.

The truck had all but disappeared—the sound of the engine fading in the night.

He kept a constant watch on the trees and the pasture while occasionally turning around to make certain the gunman hadn't come up behind him.

Several minutes passed and then more time. Worry began to set in. Where had she gone? Surely, she hadn't kept going deeper into the woods. Their plan had been to go to the cabin.

What if the man had found her? Surely, he would've heard the commotion. Josie would shoot to protect them—unless the man had snuck up on her catching her unaware.

Another glance at the woods produced no sightings of anyone.

A growl rose in the night.

Chills popped up on his arms. Heavy animal breathing accompanied the distinctive sounds. It was one thing to hear a bear on television, but quite a different story in the country at night. Was he on Josie and Everly's trail?

Dane took off through the tall grass at a run. With the gunman and the bear close by, he needed to find them quickly.

Limbs snapped and the sound of running through the trees came from his left. *Josie.* His chest grew tight with each step, and he turned toward the growing sounds.

Just as he got to the end of the pasture, a figure ran out of the forest. The gunman. The black bear was on all fours right behind him.

Dane stopped.

The gunman squealed and dropped his weapon.

He watched as the guy trekked across the pasture. After several yards, the bear stopped his pursuit to a walk, and the man kept going while looking over his shoulder.

The animal turned and put his nose into the air.

Dane stood still, holding his breath.

With a final grunt, the beast trotted back to the woods and disappeared.

It took a few seconds before he moved again. And when he did, the hamstring pain returned full force. Even though he hadn't checked the injury, he was certain it wasn't serious. More annoying than anything.

Hopefully, Josie knew to keep going, but he could only guess she had continued moving south toward the cabin. The thought that the gunman had killed Everly's dad didn't sit well in his gut. The man must've determined he had no choice but to get rid of her. Dane needed to catch up to the mother-daughter team before the killer did.

He skirted wide of the area where the bear had gone while keeping watch and picked up the rifle the man had dropped. The silhouette of the gunman could only be seen occasionally. The herd of cattle was out of view. A towering oak tree stood out from among the rest about thirty yards ahead. If he made it to that tree without seeing Josie, he would enter the woods.

As he approached the oak and didn't see her, he started to veer toward the woods.

"Where are you going?"

He flinched at the sudden female voice. Josie stepped out from behind a large bush.

"How long have you been waiting here?"

"Several minutes." She moved closer as Everly limped beside her. "When we hit the woods, we hoofed it through the trees. I heard the bear again and didn't stick around."

"I can see that. The gunman caught the bear's attention." A chuckle creeped into his voice. "Chased him for a bit."

"Really? I wished I could've witnessed that."

"The bear returned into the woods, so let's get moving."

"I heard something crash in the trees. It must've been him."

Everly walked between them with Dexter. Her limp wasn't as prominent.

"How's the ankle? Feeling better?"

"A little. It doesn't hurt as much after I walk on it."

"Would you like for me to carry you?"

The girl shook her head. Her shoulders sagged. "Nah. I'm good. Just tired."

Josie looked down at her, and he thought she was going to say something but then changed her mind. Then she glanced at him.

He mouthed, "She's okay."

Josie whispered, "I know."

But the worry lines on her face said she'd prefer it if Everly accepted help.

As they traveled, Dane kept a lookout for the bear, the gunman, and their truck. Over the next hour, there were a couple of times he thought he heard an engine in the distance, but he never saw them. At one point, Everly allowed him to carry her for a while before asking to be put back down.

Eventually, the cabin came into sight, and he put out his hand. "Wait. I want to make sure the men aren't waiting for us."

Everly dropped to the ground, folded her legs crisscross and rested her chin on her hands. Dexter lay beside her and placed his head on her lap.

They watched the home for several minutes. He finally said, "There's no sign of the truck. I think we're clear."

"Yeah, and I thought that earlier, too. But he was here waiting for us."

Dane nodded. She was right. Their man could've parked up the road or in the pasture somewhere hidden from sight. "Let me check it out. You stay here with Everly."

She reached into her pocket and pulled out her keys to her. "Here."

He took them and kept an eye out as he made his way to the yard. He skirted around her Bronco. By all appearances the men had not messed with it. He climbed in and started it. When he looked up, Josie and Everly headed his way. He got out to let her climb in. "Let me grab our suitcases."

"I'm going in with you."

She glanced over her shoulder at him but didn't comment. All three of them stuck together walking into the cabin and Dane grabbed their luggage. He didn't know how they'd left the cabin, but nothing looked out of place to him. They hurried back down the porch. Seconds later, Josie was in the driver's seat.

"Hop in the back, Everly." The girl did as she was asked.

He wanted to go with her, but he also didn't want to put her in danger. "I think I should stay here."

Josie shook her head. "Those men will be back."

"I know. But I can't have authorities searching for me."

"They're searching for you anyways. And those men just found your hiding place. I don't care what you do, but you need to make up your mind."

Everything in him told him once he was back in town, it'd be difficult to stay hidden. Headlights shone in the distance. He looked over his shoulder.

"Well?" Her eyebrows shot up.

He'd just have to find a new place. "Hit it." He hopped in.

She peeled out of the driveway and headed

down the rock road at a fast past. Her lifted vehicle sported leather seats and the engine ran smoothly. His mind whirled where she could drop him off that wouldn't compromise his safety. There was nowhere. His business partner and friend had been murdered. He'd made few friends. He'd disappointed Josie once and he didn't intend on a repeat.

If he got himself thrown in jail, she and her daughter would be on their own. He couldn't allow that to happen.

SIX

Josie made it to the highway without incident. Her mind struggled to make sense of everything. She still couldn't believe Everly had seen Pierce murdered. The police had believed it was an accident immediately, and the coroner must've agreed.

If Pierce had drowned, then surely there would've been water in his lungs. If he'd died of electrocution, burns on the skin would've been present.

A few minutes later, she glanced over the backseat and saw that Everly was slumped in her seat fast asleep. Her heart constricted. She couldn't imagine the fear she must've been going through.

"She's a sweet girl."

She glanced at Dane and took in his beard and the black T-shirt with the small hole in it. No one would've guessed he had been a business owner. Even though she'd dated him, she'd heard the rumors and insults. He was branded a bad apple, a troublemaker—someone the teachers griped openly about. His dad had spent time in prison and his mom drank a lot. He had an older brother who had gotten kicked out of school for something. For what she couldn't remember. By the time Josie came on the scene, his brother wasn't in the picture.

Even though their relationship had ended on a sour note, she still owed him appreciation. "Thank you for helping us."

"You don't have to thank me."

Other than the hum of the engine, silence filled the cab. Her lights melted into the highway. No other vehicles were in sight. Awkwardness grew. She was probably careless to take him with her since he was a wanted man, but she couldn't leave him back there with those men hunting them. Still, she had a duty to do. "I'll have to tell my boss and the sheriff about you."

Alert blue eyes glistened back at her even with the darkness of the cab. "I would expect no less. I don't suppose it matters that I didn't kill my partner."

She turned her attention back to the road. Of course, he would claim he was innocent. But he'd claimed innocence over stealing the car, too. And she'd seen that with her own eyes. "That's not my place to judge. A jury will decide."

He nodded. "Because the system always gets it right?"

Almost, yes. The system was as good as they

had. But she refused to reply to that question. She could feel his eyes on her. It was unnerving. He wasn't going to make her feel guilty. The police had tried to arrest him, and he'd run. Why would an innocent man do that? He wouldn't.

The highway dead-ended into the interstate, and she turned right toward Liberty. It was four forty-two in the morning—meaning she'd been up almost twenty-four hours. Her body was racked with exhaustion and a headache crawled from the front of her head to the back. The tree limb had almost knocked her unconscious. Dane hadn't hesitated to carry her back to his place.

Correction—his hideout.

He didn't have to help her. And he'd saved Everly from the bear. And his truck was worthless now. She tried to push the guilt aside, but it wouldn't budge. He couldn't expect her to hide a fugitive.

"Mind if I ask you something personal?"

She glanced at him and took in the seriousness of his expression. "Ask away. No guarantees, though."

"How long did it take for the adoption process for Everly?"

This was not what she expected. She scrutinized him, trying to figure out if he was attempting to divert her attention away from the talk of running from authorities.

His gaze went to the floorboard.

Because she had dreamed about having a family for years, when Everly's single dad died and there was the first mention of the state taking conservatorship, she'd moved quickly. She didn't want the girl to go into foster care if she could help it.

She'd met Everly a couple of times and had taken to her immediately. But still, Josie was protective over Everly and didn't like to talk about her adoption. Josie remembered after her family died and her grandfather took her in, people would ask her about her *real* parents. The constant reminder that her granddad wasn't "real" frustrated her. And it was like everything else that used to make her *her* had taken a backseat to the fire or what it was like to be raised by her grandfather. Almost like it changed her identity. In her previous school, she'd played tennis, was the first-string pitcher in softball, and her team had gone to state in volleyball. Because Liberty was smaller, only track, basketball, and drill team were offered for females. Her mom had also been teaching Josie and her sister to quilt. Josie had won a blue ribbon at the 4-H fair.

She had struggled to fit in and didn't want to see that happen to Everly, starting with not subjecting her to going on about the adoption. "Four months."

He frowned and mumbled, "That's not much time."

"What does that mean? Time for what?"

"Nothing." He shook his head. "I know you have other things on your mind, like getting Everly back to Liberty and going to the police."

He was right, of course. But still, he bugged her. Why would Dane Haggerty want to know about adoption? Surely, with him being a fugitive he wasn't thinking of adopting a child. "Spill it, Dane."

He turned to her, amusement dancing in his eyes, and then he sobered. "Violet, my sister. She's being taken away by the courts. For now, she's in foster care. Don't laugh, but I want to raise her."

"I would never laugh at that." She could see by his expression, he was serious. Josie barely remembered his curly-haired little sister. When she'd dated Dane, he lived with his maternal grandmother and then moved in with a neighbor. He'd talked of Violet often. "How old is she now?"

He worked his jaw. "Thirteen."

"Wow. I can't believe it. She was practically a baby when we were in school." As the hum of the tires on the pavement filled the silence, Josie realized he was done with the subject. A pang in her heart made it difficult to swallow. That was the age she'd been when her family died. She couldn't imagine being in foster care at such a fragile age. He had been enamored with his younger sister, so she didn't know why it surprised her he wanted to adopt her. But could he really offer her a better life?

She glanced his way and caught him fidgeting with his jeans. Violet was a difficult subject for him, but she had the feeling he hadn't made the decision lightly.

"You can quit staring at me. I don't want to go to prison for a crime I didn't commit, but I also have things I want to live for. That shouldn't shock you."

It was like he'd read her mind. Even though he had a reckless nature, she'd always believed Dane Haggerty had a soft heart. "You…" She swallowed. "You'll make a great dad."

To her surprise, she meant it.

He turned to her. "I hope so. I pray about it every day."

The pink of morning showed in her rearview mirror as she was about ten miles outside of Liberty. They stopped at an all-night gas station, and she filled up with gas and picked up a burner phone that she used to call her boss, Bliss.

"Hello."

"Bliss, it me, Josie."

"What's going on? I know it must be important for you to call this early. I thought you were on a camping trip."

She drew a deep breath, still debating whether to tell her about Dane. "I realize you're busy but thought you would want to know what's going on.

Everly and I were attacked last night. Long story short, after being chased through the woods by a guy with a gun, Everly admitted she witnessed her father's murder, and this guy threatened her. He's been following her ever since and finally caught up to her on our trip."

"Oh my! What a horrible thing to witness! I'm so sorry. Poor girl. I had thought Pierce died of an accident."

"Me too."

"Have you talked with law enforcement yet?"

"I'm going to call them as soon as I hang up from you. I lost my phone and just now picked up a new one."

There was a second of silence. "You know I'm in San Antonio on Mitchell's case, or I'd drive up. If you need help, call Chandler or Kennedy. Annie and Riggs are working on a case right now."

"I will. Have you learned anything valuable?"

"It looks promising. But I want you to get protection for you and your daughter. This is not the time to be alone."

Josie cringed inwardly and took a deep breath. "I will not be alone. If you need help once this thing with Everly is cleared up, give me a holler."

After they disconnected, she glanced over to Dane and their eyes met.

"I didn't ask you not to tell your boss about me."

"I know. And I would've given her more details if she didn't have important things going on in her life."

"Important case?"

"The most important case of her life. I don't suppose you've heard of Bliss Walker. Well, now her name is Bliss Adcock. She got married last year to a Texas Ranger."

He shook his head. "I know you try to find missing children."

"Bliss is the founder of our group. Years ago, while working for the US Marshals, her husband was killed in a car accident, and her son went missing from the wreckage. After years of searching for and not finding her son, she took early retirement and created the Bring the Children Home Project. Last year, her son's remains were found. A couple of weeks ago, a similar case happened where an FBI agent's wife was killed in an obvious hit-and-run just as the agent was narrowing in on a suspect in a drug smuggling ring. The same suspect Bliss had been working. I don't know all the details, but it sounds like the two may be connected." Josie prayed Bliss found closure and the persons responsible for their deaths were brought to justice.

"Oh, that's tough. I'll pray they find who was behind it."

Was Dane for real? He rarely mentioned God or prayed back when they dated except when he visited worship services with her. She mainly believed he went with her just to have more time with her. But there was no benefit to having an in-depth conversation with him. She wasn't looking to rekindle an old flame.

She hated to drop him off at the sheriff's department, but she firmly believed in the law and doing the right thing. As they neared town, she needed to make up her mind.

"You can drop me off anywhere out here."

"What?" She turned to him and could see he was serious. "The law is hunting you, and now a killer may also be after you."

He stared. "Thanks. I won't need anyone's help."

"There's no need in getting an attitude with me. You chose to run from the law. That wasn't my fault."

"You would've, too, if someone would've framed you."

"That's where you're wrong." She pointed a finger at him. "I would trust the law officers to do their job."

"Oh, how the girl from high school who finished in the top of our class and whose granddad was in law enforcement thinks she knows everything about the rest of us."

"I worked hard in school."

"So did I. Kindly pull over at the next road and let me out."

She shook her head. "No. You need to set this straight."

"If you don't pull over, I'll jump out."

Her gaze went to his hand on the door handle and then back to his dark steely eyes as they locked onto her—daring her to doubt his resolve. He'd always been willing to take risks. "You haven't changed a bit, Dane Haggerty."

"Actually, I have. But I'm not about to go down for a crime I didn't commit. Not when a young girl is depending on me."

The Bronco came to a stop on the shoulder of the road. Everly sat up in the back seat. "What's going on?"

"Take care, Everly," he said as he exited the vehicle. His gaze went from Everly back to Josie. Before he slammed the door, he said, "I'm sorry it had to end this way."

"Why are we leaving him?" Everly leaned over the seat, resting her arm on top.

How did she answer her? Everly already had too much to worry about. "He wants me to leave him there, honey. Right now, I'm taking you home to talk with the police."

Everly stared out the back window. "But there's nothing back there. No car or house. What's he going to do?"

Her teeth ground together as she pulled away. "I'm not certain."

As Josie checked her rearview mirror, headlights came over the horizon. She kept her speed down and watched the vehicle draw closer. Suddenly, she recognized the black truck the men had driven. She stopped and put the Bronco in Reverse and floored it.

"Watch out!" Josie's warning came out as the truck whipped onto the road she'd left Dane on. He must've just noticed them, for he ran into the ditch and the truck followed.

Dane opened fire on the truck, but it kept coming. Right as it got to him, he dodged being hit by rolling back into the road and lying flat on his belly.

Josie turned onto the road just as a grain dump truck came from the other direction straight at Dane.

Everly yelled, "No!"

Dane ducked his head as the grain truck appeared to run over him.

Josie's heart stopped. The large vehicle halted in the middle of the road, its engine humming.

Meanwhile, the black truck continued into the ditch and then pulled back onto the road going in the other direction.

She stopped on the shoulder, got out and ran to Dane, who was on the other side of the grain truck.

His hands covered his head. Slowly, he looked up at her. "I'm still alive?"

"You won't be for long if we don't get you out of here." She bent over and gave him a hand up.

"What are you doing?" The driver of the grain truck hurried his way. "I almost killed you."

"I'm glad you didn't." Dane shot him a smile as Josie hurried him toward her vehicle.

As soon as he was back in, she pointed her finger at him. "Don't ever threaten to pull such a dangerous stunt on me again, or I'll…" Everly's eyes grew large from the backseat, and Josie warned, "Just don't."

"I would've waited for you to slow a little." He smiled.

"I don't care." She hoped her voice conveyed the seriousness she intended.

"Understood. Now let me go from here."

She shook her head, but then she knew he was right. He wouldn't allow her to take him to the sheriff's department, but it wouldn't be smart for her to know where he was going. "Okay."

He hurried into the adjoining pasture. He took off at a jog, and she watched him disappear into some trees. When she was satisfied he was out of sight and the men's truck hadn't returned, she got back on the road.

"I don't know why you let him go." Everly frowned.

"There are things you don't understand." But as Josie got her speed up on the highway, Dane's words replayed through her mind. *I don't sup-*

pose it matters that I didn't kill my partner. If he didn't, then he had nothing to hide. Why run? Especially now that he knew the man who had targeted them at the cabin was also after him?

Her phone rang and Bliss's name showed on the screen. "This is Josie."

"I talked with Sheriff Van Carroll. He's out of town but he's sending a deputy to meet you at your house, and Chandler should be giving you a call."

"I plan to do more research on the victim to find potential suspects." Josie purposely didn't mention Pierce's name in front of Everly. Bliss had a great working relationship with the sheriff, so she appreciated her making the call. "The sooner we find this guy, the better."

"I agree."

"I know. Thanks." After she disconnected, she turned on the white rock road to her house. The older farmhouse sat in the middle of a large pasture, with only a scattering of trees. The home was fashioned as a Queen Anne Victorian, but much smaller than most with only a single-story and a wrap-around porch.

Everly's bike leaned against the white fence. The front porch light was on, but the rest of the house was dark—just the way she'd left it. Neither the deputy nor Chandler was here yet. She pulled across the cattle guard and kept an eye out for anything out of the ordinary. The door-less garage sat ten yards from the home, and she drove inside. "We're home."

"Will we be safe here?"

Josie gave her what she hoped was a reassuring smile. "Yes. But remember to let me know anything—" how to say it? "—anything that happens that I need to know about. Please don't be nervous confiding in me."

"Okay." Everly got out of the back seat. Dexter leaped down after her.

Josie grabbed their bags as Everly and the dog ran up the steps to the back porch. Her daughter retrieved the keys from under the ceramic frog. As she thought about Pierce's killer following Everly for months, it suddenly dawned on her that he would know where they lived. She dropped the bags. "Everly, wait!"

But she'd already opened the door and disappeared inside.

Josie was hurrying up the steps when Everly screamed. Her heart constricted at the sound as she removed her Sig from her pocket and stepped inside.

Crying reached her as she ran to the back of her house to Everly's room. Her daughter wrapped her arms around herself. Her teddy bear was lying on the bed with a piece of cloth wrapped around its mouth and a note pinned to it.

* * *

Dane made tracks through the woods and came out on the other side—where the backyard of a modest brick house blended into the morning sunrise. He shielded his eyes as he strode to the residence. A tabby cat jumped from a planter's box in the window and followed him around the front of the home. Before he could rap on the door, it opened.

"Dane Haggerty. It's good of you to drop by. Haven't seen you in forever."

He hated to involve this woman, but he had little choice. "I need help, Nellie."

The older lady waved him in. "Come on in."

Nellie Hickman had cleaned North Texas Custom Builder's offices twice a week since the day they opened. Harlan had known the woman for years before then. "I guess you haven't heard."

The woman wore an apron that read *Never Trust a Skinny Chef.* "I hear things all the time. That doesn't mean I believe them."

He looked up into kind eyes. "That means a lot to me."

"Have you eaten breakfast?"

He'd skipped supper last night but didn't want to stay longer than necessary. "I don't want to bring trouble to your door. I need a ride."

She folded her arms across her chest and stared at him for several seconds as if in thought. "Come with me."

Dane followed her out the back door to the garage. A large beige tarp lay on top of a couple of vehicles, and she peeled it off to reveal an old classic blue pickup. He let out a whistle. "That's nice, but I couldn't…"

"I wasn't offering it to you." She smiled. "My father-in-law bought this new in 1962 and my Roger restored it. I ain't gettin' no younger and figure it's about time I drive it." She jerked her head at the other vehicle. "That one is for you."

A four-door silver sedan that was probably fifteen years old, and the paint was beginning to fade was parked beside the truck. Nellie tossed Dane the keys. He admitted this vehicle would bring him less attention, which was what he needed.

"You don't have to do this."

"I know it. Bring it back to me when you're done with it."

"I will."

"It won't do you no good to leave here on an empty stomach. Come in and I'll fix you some bacon and eggs. Won't take five minutes and I don't want no argument."

Dane followed the lady back instead.

"Fishing has been good this year. Have you been?"

"A couple of times. Caught me a large catfish." Even though he was on the run, it was important to blend in. He'd gone fishing on a stock tank on the land where he'd stayed.

The woman's bright eyes glistened. "It's been a while since I had fish fry. Alec hasn't had much time to go this year. You need to stop by later, and we'll have one." She started frying bacon while she talked, and then cracked some eggs in a bowl where she gave them a quick whisk. Soon, she had them in a separate pan.

"I'd like that. Let's plan on it." Alec was Nellie's son who'd worked for Harlan and him a while back before they had to let him go due to problems with alcohol. It was a shame, too, because Nellie was a gem. Back when Dane was young, Nellie often gave him odd jobs to do around the yard and always paid. That might seem small to some people, but for Dane, who had little spending money, it had meant the world.

True to her word, Nellie had the food ready in minutes. She handed him the meal on a paper plate with a plastic fork and knife, along with coffee in a foam cup. "Have a good day. I hope you can get the business back up and running soon."

"Me too. Thank you." Dane settled into the sedan and put his food in the console, then pulled out of the driveway. There were few people he could depend on, and appreciation for the older woman grew.

He turned left onto the highway—the opposite direction Josie had gone. He had to stay in hiding. Josie had worked with the sheriff's department and now with the Bring Home the Children Project, which employed many with backgrounds in law enforcement. She would be in good hands. Much better than Dane was.

Time was closing in on getting custody of Violet. It may already be too late because he'd have to prove his innocence and then that he could be a suitable parent. Being a fugitive made it almost impossible.

He needed to go to his office to see if any evidence had been missed. Driving Nellie's car, he had to be careful. He didn't want to get her in trouble in case he was pulled over or caught. Although unlikely, he didn't want to take the chance of her being charged as an accomplice. He figured she'd play ignorant of his runaway status, though, if questioned, just as she had with him. Anyone seeing her car at the office would assume she was working.

The sun shone bright and summer flowers were in bloom. Everything seemed normal, completely unlike his world, which had been turned upside down.

His office building sat on a county highway. Not expensive real estate, but in an easy to get to location. It was nine thirty in the morning with the normal business traffic of work pickups, semitrucks and a variety of other vehicles. As he neared his office, the neighboring business, Kountry Kuts, had three cars parked out front, and the heavy equipment rental place had several pickups in the parking lot.

His foot eased off the gas as he passed North Texas Custom Builders. No vehicles were parked out front, and a closed sign stood in the window. He continued past and drove to the next road about a half mile down. After turning around, he kept a lookout for anyone suspicious who could be looking for him, but he saw no one. Maybe in the months he'd been in hiding, the authorities or bounty hunters had quit staking out the place. Instead of going slow, he blended in with the traffic and then pulled around to the back.

With a quick glance, he climbed out of Nellie's sedan and strode to the back door. He put his key in, half expecting it not to work, but it turned. From the terms of their partnership, Harlan's widow would inherit half of the business. He stepped in and when he tried the lights, they came on. That was good. He'd done research to find out what would happen to the business should he be arrested, and from what he found, the company would be in the hands of the court. All assets would be sold, and profits would pay off the debts. Harlan's widow could buy out Dane's half. The court date had not appeared online yet.

A quick walkthrough of the downstairs showed no change except the surfaces were now dusty. Hurriedly he went up the metal stairs to his office where he had found Harlan on the floor. The bloodstains had been cleaned and the murder weapon—his granddad's hay hook—was not there. Not that he expected it to be. It was surreal looking at the business he and Harlan had worked hard to build and knowing his partner was gone and he was on the run for his murder. Their business would be dissolved. Or maybe bought by someone else. The scripture in Luke came to him that talked about a man building bigger barns to lay up treasures, but in the end, the man died. God asked who shall receive those things you have provided. As much as it made his gut tighten, Dane didn't like the thought of someone else receiving everything he and Harlan had worked for.

No doubt the police had gone through the desk and file cabinets searching for evidence. But he glanced through the paperwork anyway. Maybe something had been overlooked that only Dane would recognize.

Why had someone gone to the trouble to frame him? If it had been a simple robbery, they could've killed Harlan and run. And why use his grandfather's hay hook? Maybe the killer hadn't come with the intent to murder his partner and didn't know it belonged to him. But he didn't think so.

As these thoughts came to him, he knew he must search fast. A stack of bills was piled on the corner of the desk, and he quickly sifted through them. Besides utility and mortgage information, the only other bills were for contractors they'd used. The large desk calendar in the center of the desktop was still on the date four months prior. A quick glance at the couple of weeks before showed three deadlines for bids on upcoming jobs and several dates for completion of jobs. As always, the completion of jobs could vary depending upon a number of factors, but Harlan used a color-coded system to indicate early, goal, and last possible dates. He'd been a stickler for being on time, something their customers often commented on.

Everything looked in order on the calendar with no unknown names or appointments to draw suspicions. Next, he went through the filing cabinets. Even though the computers were used for records, Harlan liked to have a hard copy of important documents. Dane scanned them quickly and disappointment hit him when nothing presented itself as unusual.

He put his hands on his hips and glanced around the room. Some people brought work home with them, but Harlan used to advise Dane to draw a line between work and family. His partner worked long hours, but when he left for the day, work stayed here.

But did Harlan ever take things home? Was there some clue at his home office? Possibly. Especially since the money missing from their business later turned up in his account. Dane had met Layla, Harlan's widow, on numerous occasions, but most conversations had simply been quick small talk.

Had there been something Dane had missed the days before the murder? The trash cans were empty. The murder happened on a Tuesday. Nellie cleaned on Monday and Thursday nights so that would make sense. And since Dane had found Harlan a little past seven in the morning, there'd be nothing in the receptacles.

Again, the place on the floor where Harlan's body had been lying caught his attention. He couldn't believe his friend was really gone. More like he'd left on a vacation and would be back in a couple of days.

Harlan had been an inspirational man.

Dane felt bad for not visiting Layla. After Harlan's first wife died, he married Layla—a woman eighteen years his junior—but that was before Dane knew him. Over a year ago, the accountant, Jim Price, who helped do the books for North Texas Custom Builders moved to the Dallas metroplex, and even though Layla retired from being a personal secretary to a CEO of an oil company, she showed no interest in helping with their company. Harlan tried to keep up with ledgers, and only hired Jim before tax season.

Harlan's twin daughters from his first marriage

were at Baylor College, one for a BA in communications and the other a BS in biochemistry. Harlan talked about his daughters often and went to many of the college's events. With the girls away, his wife was probably lonely. He didn't know how close Layla was to her stepdaughters, being that she was only a few years older than them.

He wondered again if it was possible Harlan started taking work home with him. If so, he hadn't mentioned it.

Dane needed to get moving. He quickly went through the closets in both offices and then the tiny kitchen that contained a mini refrigerator and a microwave.

He didn't know what he was hoping to find but he was certain there had to be evidence that would exonerate him. Or at least provide another suspect.

The sound of a door slamming came from somewhere outside. He hurried to the window and looked out. A silver pickup sat in the parking lot below and two men stepped out. Dane eased to the side to avoid being spotted. All he could see from this point was the top of their cowboy hats. The man who'd driven was bulky, and the one who got out on the passenger side was younger, lanky and dark, curly hair stuck out from under his hat. His heart thumped in this chest. Who would be coming by the business? One of them gave Nellie's car a look over, and then said something to the younger one.

He needed to get out of there but if he went downstairs, he might not have time to stay hidden before they came in. Deciding to wait, he watched them, trying to learn their identities. They moved toward the back door that he'd entered, and before they disappeared under the awning, the bigger guy glanced up.

Dane jerked back and out of the way, but he didn't know if the man had spotted him.

A door slammed shut and footsteps clicked on the tile below.

He hurried into the closet and silently shut the door.

Footsteps came up the stairs. Not in a big hurry. Once they made it to the top floor, one man moved toward Dane's office.

Anger burned his insides as he thought about someone invading his personal space. The construction company was his and Harlan's. It'd been bought with hard work and sacrifice. Eager to learn the man's identity, Dane eased the door open a crack and peeked out. The older man's back was to him. But there was something familiar about the way the fellow moved.

The other man disappeared into his office but was not quiet. A crash sounded and then papers flitted into the doorway. A deep voice mumbled, "Where did you hide it?"

More commotion as drawers slammed and then there was the playing of an oldie's tune. It was the guy's ringtone on his cell phone. "What?" After a pause, he said, "Not yet. I just got here. Give me two minutes to look and then I'll be there shortly."

Dane stayed hidden until the young man walked by. The only thing he could make out was dark curly hair, and then he disappeared into his office. There was more banging and chatter between the two men until finally the footsteps retreated downstairs.

Byron Ferguson had a stocky build like the older man. Once the door slammed, Dane came out and looked back out the window. As the truck drove off, he tried to read his license plate, but the sun reflected from the metal bumper, obscuring the view before it disappeared around the building—he only made out four numbers. He didn't recognize the vehicle, but it was new.

Byron Ferguson—his job foreman.

What was his old job foreman looking for? It had been difficult to investigate the murder while on the run. In the movies, a person always had someone on the inside willing to slip the fugitive information. But Dane had no one he could trust. Not his family, and he didn't trust his coworkers.

He moved to the door and stepped out onto the balcony. Just months before he'd jumped from this railing to the ground below and had injured his ribs.

Trust.

Harlan used to quote the proverb, *Trust in the Lord with all thine heart; and lean not unto thine own understanding.*

Trust the Lord, yes. But his ex-coworkers?

He wanted to ask Josie to run a check on their old foreman to see what he'd been doing since he left the company and where he got the money for a new vehicle. But could he trust her?

He had to take a leap of faith sometime.

SEVEN

Josie hurried across the floor and picked up the bear.

Keep your mouth shut or people will die.

What kind of sick person would leave a threatening note for a child? She wrapped her arms around her daughter and pulled her close. "I'm so sorry. No one is going to die. We're going to find this guy and he will be arrested."

"No." Everly shrugged out of her grasp. "He's going to find and kill me. Just like he did my daddy. My dad was strong, and if the bad guy could take him down, there's no way you'll be able to stop him."

Josie's heart ached at her words, and she kneeled on one knee in front of her. "I won't let that happen. Your dad must've been taken by surprise. He didn't expect an attack. But now the authorities and I are watching for this man. We'll protect you." Even as she said the words, she prayed they were true. She'd never been responsible for anyone besides herself. Well, considering she worked with teams of others who'd sworn to protect, that wasn't exactly true. But she'd never had a family of her own since she was thirteen.

Everly frowned. "I hope you're right."

A child shouldn't have to worry about such things. She should be playing hopscotch or other games with friends.

She'd learned a long time ago that doing chores and staying busy helped keep the mind occupied. "How about you put your clothes away and feed Dexter."

"Okay."

Taking the bear with her, Josie walked into the kitchen and made a call to Sheriff Van Carroll's office. "Hattie, is the sheriff available?"

"Hey, Josie. It's been a while since I heard from you."

"Yeah, it's been a few months and we should get together. But this is important. Is he available?"

The deputy's jovial tone turned serious. "No, he isn't. He got called out of town for some family thing. Speaking of, I can't wait to meet your new daughter."

Bliss had mentioned him being out of town. "I have a situation and was hoping for his assistance." She knew Bliss had reached out to his office, but she needed to make sure help was on the way.

"Is there anything I can do?"

She gave her the abbreviated version of what had happened in the past day, ending with the note attached to the bear.

"You know not to touch the note. I doubt it, but maybe the guy left his fingerprints on it."

"We touched the bear, but not the note. I would love to have a protection detail for me and Everly."

"Oh, you know what? According to this message on my desk, Bliss already called. Deputy Green must have taken the call while I was on break. We're stretched tight, but I'll get the word to one of the deputies or will help you myself. You know, a wellness check on your place may be the best we can do."

"Thanks, Hattie. I'm going to dive into Pierce's case and see what I can find. Makes me wonder if he was investigating something that got him killed."

A creak sounded behind her.

She cringed when she turned to see Everly staring at her and holding the dog food scoop. "I'll be in touch." She disconnected the phone and said, "Do you need help feeding Dexter?"

"His bowl is in the Bronco. I thought maybe you wanted to get it for me. Do you think Daddy's killer was somebody who worked with him?"

"It's possible." Josie hadn't gotten used to someone being in her house every minute and how easy it was for her daughter to overhear her conversations. "Did your dad mention anyone by name?"

Everly shook her head. "Not that I remember."

"Did he talk about the cases he was working?"

"Sometimes." She shrugged. "It mainly depends. One time he was paid to track down a lady's missing cat named Percy that ran away during a thunderstorm. He found her two weeks later in a shed in the backyard. Percy had five kittens."

Josie smiled. "Let me get Dexter's bowl for you."

She placed the stuffed animal in a gallon plastic bag, being careful not to touch the note. As Everly followed her out the back door to the porch, she grabbed his feeding container from her SUV and brought it to her. It didn't hit her until now that Everly must have been afraid to go outside by herself with her dad's killer threatening her. Her gaze went to Everly's bicycle leaning against the fence. Josie had bought it for her since the girl's aunt had disposed of her other bike. She had assumed Everly never rode it because she was depressed. Now it made sense.

"Daddy talked on the phone a lot and I wasn't supposed to listen, but sometimes I heard him anyway."

Josie stopped and looked at her. Her head hung

down, but she stared up with her brown eyes like what she had to say was important.

"Did you hear anything lately?"

"Maybe. He talked with a woman named Nellie. There were others, but I can't remember anything specific. I wish I could remember more."

Nellie wasn't a common name around Liberty. The only Nellie that Josie knew was a woman who worked in billing for a rural trash service. "That's okay. But if you recall anything else, can you let me know?"

A vehicle sounded out front. Josie looked around the corner to see a Jarvis County Sheriff's SUV pull into the drive and stop in front of them. Deputy Green got out.

"Are you okay, Josie? Bliss called earlier and said someone shot at you?"

"Yeah. I called Hattie a few minutes ago. I have something for you. Hold on." She hurried inside and retrieved the bear. After she handed him the stuffed animal, she explained about it being left in Everly's room.

He asked several more questions and typed her answers into an electronic device. A voice came over his radio. He stepped away and answered it. A minute later, he was back. "I have another call I need to take. We're a little shorthanded, but we'll continue to check on you."

"Thanks."

After Dexter was fed and watered, Josie asked

Everly to stay inside. She didn't want her outdoors, even though they lived in the country in a safe area. She set the suitcase on her bed in her room but hurried to get on her laptop. She could put her clothes away later.

The first thing she did was call and request the coroner's report on Pierce's death. Then she scrolled back through her texts to the last time she'd talked with Everly's dad. Every so often they'd share information or discuss a case, but her last contact was over seven months ago—three months before his death. He had texted her stating his old pair of night vision goggles were scratched and out of date and asked which night vision optics she recommended. And the text prior to that one was when he'd invited her to his Independence Day party almost a year ago.

That was as far back as the texts went. She'd gotten a new number when she resigned from the sheriff's department and started her own private investigator company while volunteering with the Bring Home the Children Project. If only they had talked more recently, maybe she could've had a clue as to who his clients were. Getting access to his files now would be more complicated. After the adoption was finalized, Everly had come to live with her and had brought several boxes of items with her. The rest of Pierce Browning's belongings had been either sold or donated by Pierce's sister who lived in Florida.

Much of the family's savings had been wiped out due to his wife's illness several years prior, and Pierce had taken out a second mortgage on their home. Basically, it went back to the bank at his death. Pierce and his wife had set up a prepaid tuition plan for college that Everly could use when she became eighteen.

The rest of Pierce's living extended family were either elderly or not interested in raising a young girl.

Where would his work files have been stored? What had happened to his laptop? Josie still hadn't gone through the boxes, but maybe Everly knew what had been packed.

"Everly, come here please."

Seconds later, she came into the room. "Yeah?"

"Do you know what happened to your dad's things? Like his laptop or business files?"

She shrugged, and her gaze went to the floor. "I dunno. After his death, I stayed with my aunt until you adopted me. My aunt and uncle went to our house, but they made me stay in the car while they loaded up his things they said I would want."

The girl wouldn't look at her. "Honey, is there something you want to tell me? Have you looked through the boxes?"

"I don't want to lie." Her frown deepened. "I went through them once."

"You're not in trouble." Josie sighed. She wished Everly would've told her. Josie had no idea what her aunt thought the girl needed to keep. Irritation crawled all over her. She wasn't an expert on the law, but Everly should've inherited all of her parents' things. Poor child. And Josie had considered looking through boxes but had put it off because she hadn't found the time. Life had been a whirlwind of activity since Everly moved in.

"Aunt Ruby told me not to go through his things, that it was best to move on with my new life."

"Oh, honey. His things belong to you. I wouldn't have minded." Josie desperately wanted to wrap her in a hug, but that tended to make Everly shy away. She settled for a hand on her shoulder. "Grief takes a while. I lost my family when I was a child and I still miss them every day."

Everly cocked her head at her. "What happened?"

A lump formed in Josie's throat. Rarely did she talk about that night even to this day. If only she hadn't been pouting because her parents told her she couldn't have a friend over, she would've been on the first floor and could've saved them. "Our house caught on fire. They weren't able to get out." She could still see their faces today. But as time went on, their faces began to blur and that scared her.

"Did you have brothers and sisters?"

"I had a younger sister. Audrey."

"I'm sorry. I always wanted a sister. Were you the only who got out of the fire?"

"Yes." Josie forced a smile past the emotion that bubbled inside of her. She didn't want to talk about the fire. Or her family. "Do you mind if we look through the boxes?"

"I would love to."

"Okay. I don't know if we can make it through all of them, but we can get started."

Everly moved quickly out the door, but then turned back. "I'm sorry about your family." Then she hurried toward the detached garage.

A lump formed in Josie's throat. Somehow Everly's condolences meant more than she believed possible. She drew a deep breath before performing a quick survey around the place to make certain there were no signs of the men who'd attacked them. Her gun rested safely in her pocket. Satisfied no one was lurking, they entered the door to the storage room at the back of the garage. A variety of unmarked boxes and tubs were stacked in the corner. For the moment, Josie was only interested in finding Pierce's laptop and work files, but she stood back while Everly opened the first container.

The girl's face wrinkled into a frown.

Josie moved closer and glanced inside. A pile of shirts and ties were stuffed inside. When Everly pulled out one of the ties, several shirts fell out onto the concrete floor. She quickly picked up a sweatshirt and held it against her face. Then she paused and looked up at Josie. "This was one of his favorites." She held up the faded and soft shirt showing the logo of Browning Investigations printed on it. "He said my mom bought it for him a long time ago. One time when we were camping, he let me wear it when I got cold."

"That was kind of him. I know you miss your dad." From what Josie witnessed, Pierce was a loving father. "Would you like to take that one in the house with us?"

"Yeah." Everly glanced down. "But I lost my butterfly necklace that Daddy gave me on my last birthday. I'm sorry."

"Oh no, honey. I should've told you. I found it in the woods last night dangling from a tree. The chain is broken, but I'll get it repaired as soon as possible."

Her mouth dropped open. "Thank you! When Daddy gave it to me he told me to take good care of it."

Josie patted her on the back. Then she looked up at the dozen or so containers and knew it would take a while to sift through them. She needed to find his records now.

"Would it be all right if I bring this in?" Everly held up a man's baseball cap.

"Certainly. You don't have to ask. These items are yours." The only thing she would prefer was for Everly not to find something personal or too stressful for a girl of her age to see. Josie grabbed the next container, which held a stack of photograph albums and pictures. She shoved it over to Everly. While her daughter went through those, she quickly opened four more before finding one that contained mail, electronics and things that looked to be from his office. "Do you mind if I take this one inside so I can go through it?"

Everly nodded. "Sure. And I'd like to take the pictures to my room."

They hurried into the house, each carrying a box. Everly disappeared into her room while Josie unpacked her box on the dining room table. Bingo. At the bottom was his laptop. A few minutes later, she had it plugged in and charging. When the screen lit up, it asked for a password. She tried several common variations containing family names and birthdates. When that didn't work, she hollered at Everly.

"Yeah?"

"Do you know your dad's password for his computer?"

She shrugged. "I'm not sure."

"What did he call your mom?"

"Her name was Melody, but he called her Mel."

"Okay. Thanks." Josie tried multiple combinations and finally, "Melsguy" worked. The computer powered opened. Several of the programs were the same as Josie used and she was thankful. She opened an Excel sheet titled Browning Investigation Clients. That made it easy.

She scrolled to the bottom of the list. Her heart picked up the pace. The last name was Harlan Schmidt, Dane's business partner.

Pierce had been investigating Dane's construction business. Was it just a coincidence Dane was in the woods where they had rented the cabin? She'd been deceived by him before. Did she dare take a chance on him again?

Suddenly an engine rumbled up her driveway. A glance out the window showed Dane riding his motorcycle. Time to make a decision had just run out.

EIGHT

As Dane cut the engine on his motorcycle, he saw Josie coming out the back door and onto the porch. He put the kickstand down and hurried her way.

"What is it?"

"I got a hunch." At her raised eyebrows in question, he continued. "I went by my office today at the construction business…"

"Yeah…" Impatience radiated from her tone. "And where did you get the motorcycle?"

"It's mine. It was in the barn with my old pickup. I borrowed a car from the woman who cleaned our offices and drove back out to the barn and exchanged it for this. She's one of the few people I trust. Anyway, I got a hunch. I definitely believe Harlan's murder and Everly's dad's murder may be connected. While I was at the office, I'm ninety percent certain Byron Ferguson, our job foreman, came by. I could only read four of the numbers on his license plate. Can you run it for me?" He removed a piece of paper from his shirt pocket and handed it to her.

She glanced at it. "I'll see what I can do. What did he want?"

Dane shrugged. "I didn't find out because I hid. And there was a younger man with him I didn't recognize. I figure it's better not to trust anyone until I learn who killed Harlan. I know this is shaky ground with you working for the Bring the Children Home Project and often with law enforcement, but can you check out some people for me? I'd never ask this if it weren't important." He hated requesting this of her. She'd trusted him once and believed he'd let her down. "If the same person who killed Harlan also killed Pierce, then we could be helping each other."

"I think you're right."

His defensiveness fell. "You do?"

She nodded. "I found some of Pierce's notes. Harlan's name was listed as one of his clients—his last client."

For the first time in months, Dane's heart lifted. Almost afraid to hope, he asked, "What did it say he was investigating? Did it give names or conclusions on what he found?"

She put up her hand. "Not so fast. I haven't had time to go over everything. All I know is Harlan's name was the last on the list. It stands to reason there's a connection. But I need to let the authorities know. Turn yourself in and that way we can look into the cases without worrying about you being arrested."

He sighed. "I'm going to repeat myself. I did not steal that car in high school, but it did not stop me from going into juvenile detention. I don't trust law enforcement. It's easy for you. You were not judged because of your family."

She frowned, frustration showing on her face, and then she turned and walked toward the house. "If you weren't guilty of stealing, then why were you in Principal Scruggs's car? The police said someone kicked in his back door and stole the Mustang's keys before taking the car. For an innocent guy, you sure did a terrific job making yourself look guilty."

He followed her as she kept talking.

"You were hot rodding and ran his car on two wheels. Not exactly the actions of someone trying to avoid trouble." She took a deep breath. "But you're not a kid anymore and you ran a thriving business. They'll believe you. And the evidence should be lacking."

"I did not kick in Scruggs's door, but it was part of the lie that was repeated. Seems like no one questioned the other kids or considered one of them may have broken into the principal's house. It did no good to say it, though. Even *you* believed the lie. And if they don't believe me this time?"

"Trust in the system."

Nope. He wasn't going to do it. He reached out for her hand to get her to stop walking. "I have Violet to think about. I'm her last hope."

"Instead of letting the authorities investigate, you'd rather live as a fugitive?" She pulled away. "Being on the run raises your chances of something going wrong. You'll have no protection if this guy comes after you. You could easily lose your life."

Again, he reached for her, but his hand just managed to snag her shirt, which tugged up a little on the side. A terrible pink scar showed. "What is that?"

"Nothing." She yanked her shirt down.

"Is that what I think it is?" Disbelief hit him. He could tell by her flaring eyes it was true. "You took a bullet? Was it serious?"

"Aren't they all?"

"You know what I mean."

She looked thoughtful for a moment. "Yeah. It was. I suppose that's the closest I've ever come to death."

He couldn't believe she hadn't mentioned being shot before. "Who did this? When did this happen?"

"Last year when I was helping Chandler Murphy bring home a missing child. I was shot."

A door slammed, and he turned to see Everly standing on the steps with Dexter at her side. The frown she wore told him she'd overheard the last comment.

"Everly." Josie hurried her way.

Her eyebrows furrowed into a frown. "I don't want you to be hurt, Mom. I don't want to lose you."

"Oh, honey." Josie knelt in front of her and placed her hands on her shoulders. "I didn't mean for you to overhear that."

Dane stood where he was, giving them room. He never should've come by here. "I'll be going now."

He waited for Josie to argue and tell him to stay, but she just stared at him. "I'll contact you if I learn anything."

As he climbed on his motorcycle, Dexter ran over barking at him and Everly followed. Dane flicked his hand at the dog. He didn't know if he was more upset about finding out Josie had taken a bullet last year or that Everly had overheard. All he knew was he needed to find out who was targeting them and put an end to this madness. He looked at the collie. "Stay back, boy."

"I don't want you to go. Stay here." The girl's brown eyes stared up at him, which reminded him so much of Violet.

Dane shot her a smile. If only Josie wanted him to stay, then they could work together to find out who framed him. "I'll be fine."

Josie called with a frustrated expression, "Come on in, and we'll get something to eat."

Even though he was still hungry after the breakfast Nellie had made for him, he didn't want to stay if she didn't want him there. "I don't want to intrude. I understand I've put you in a bad position."

Josie shook her head. "I wouldn't offer if it wasn't okay." She turned and walked to the house.

Everly came up beside him. "I like your motorcycle. I wish I had one."

"You have to be very careful, but maybe your mom will allow me to give you a ride sometime."

She shrugged. "Maybe."

When he came into the kitchen a few moments later, Josie was hurriedly setting out the fixings for sandwiches. He opened the cabinet door closest to the sink and found the glasses then put them on the counter. "Everly, what would you like to drink?"

"Milk. But I can get it." She grabbed the jug, and he filled his glass with water from the refrigerator dispenser.

"I'll take milk, too," Josie said to Everly, then turned her attention to him. "Thanks."

He took in the red face and quick movements, telling him she was frustrated. "Welcome."

They all sat at the table and then Josie said, "Everly, would you like to say the blessing?"

"Sure." The girl's gaze met his before she bowed her head and said grace.

It was odd because growing up, his family never prayed. It wasn't until he met Harlan that Dane had seriously considered God and prayer. He had to admit he was glad Josie and Everly had faith.

Everyone helped themselves to make their own sandwiches and grab chips. They remained quiet while they were eating; evidently everyone was hungry or too distracted to talk.

Dane knew he'd eaten too fast, but he was certain the food would catch up soon and he'd regret it if he ate more. He pushed back from the table. "That was good. I didn't realize how hungry I was."

Josie smiled as she finished the last bite of her sandwich. "Me either."

Everly glanced at them and seemingly understood they needed to be alone. "I'm going to my room."

"Leave the door cracked, please."

Everly stared at her mom. "I will."

Ever since her family perished in the fire, she couldn't relax if the bedroom doors were closed. Technically, it was safer to cut back on oxygen to control a fire by keeping doors closed, but Josie feared not knowing if one broke out. She'd told Everly the rule, but not the reason. It was probably time she explained.

After Everly had left the kitchen, Josie started clearing the table. "I need to be more careful when talking around her because she overhears a lot. I think she may be trying to figure out what is going on and purposely listening in."

"Wouldn't it be better if you had her shut her bedroom door then?"

Josie shook her head. "No, I like to be able to see where she's at."

"Any particular reason?"

Her head jerked. "I just do."

There was more to her statement. Much more. He remembered Josie had been extra careful about fires back when they dated. Things like unplugging cords from wall outlets and refusing to use space heaters ever. It wouldn't be such a big deal, but when he lived with a neighbor during his junior year, a single space heater was all they had to heat with. A glance at the living room wall showed a smoke alarm, and there was one in the hallway he could see. "I thought it was safer to leave doors shut."

Her gaze connected with his. "I realize this."

He was glad she didn't pretend not to know what he was referring to.

She cleared her throat. "The sheriff won't be back for a couple of days. I know many of the deputies, but the ones on duty haven't been with the department for long. And with the annual July Fourth jamboree taking place at the fairgrounds with the rodeo, they're shorthanded. We haven't been hit since we've been home, but I don't want to be a sitting duck."

"I agree. I'll help watch over you two."

She smiled. "I appreciate that. Being that Harlan appears to be Pierce's last client, I'd like to check out his office. Do you think that's possible?"

"Sure."

"What is it?" She looked at him curiously.

"I don't know what you're talking about."

"That smile. What's going on?"

He shook his head. "You're asking to look for evidence in the case. I know you're investigating because of Pierce, but I've been on my own for the past few months while trying to stay hidden. I would've done anything to have someone examine the facts with me. It's a resounding yes that you check out the office."

She nodded. "You're not afraid of what I might find?"

"Not hardly." Even if she didn't fully believe him, maybe she would come around once she saw for herself that he was innocent. "What about Everly? Is there anyone she can stay with?"

Josie's face etched in concern. "I could let my granddad watch her, if necessary, but I don't want to alarm him. I'd rather her stay by my side."

"I hate to ask, but…do you think she could look at mug shots? If we could learn who killed her dad, authorities could arrest him. And it'd make it easier to clear my name."

"Let me pray on it. I realize the best thing for her would be to know this man can't reach any of us."

"Okay. You're her mom."

She gave him a double take. Was it his imagination or was she extra sensitive concerning her daughter?

"I'm ready to go when you are," he said.

She looked thoughtful. "I'm trying to make up my mind whether we should wait until dark or not."

"Good question. I don't want to be spotted, so my vote is to wait." At her annoyed look, he wished he'd kept his mouth shut. He knew she didn't like helping him hide. Not that he blamed her, but from here on out he wouldn't mention it.

"Come on back." She jerked her head toward the table in the living room. "Remind me of the name of your foreman again?"

"Byron Ferguson."

"Hold on." She typed fast onto her cell phone. "I sent Chandler his name. I talked to him earlier, and he said he'd be glad to look at some suspects."

He stood at her side as she sat in the chair and typed on the laptop. A list of names came up on an Excel sheet. "Is Chandler an investigator?"

Without looking up, she shook her head. "He

works with the K-9 unit for the sheriff's department and for our team. But we all help each other out when possible."

What must it be like to be a part of a team with people like Josie? She seemed to be comfortable with her career choice. He didn't like the idea of her being in dangerous situations where she could be shot, but he believed the mission of her team was important.

He knew when he'd met her as a teen that she would do something important with her life.

She scrolled down the Excel sheet. Harlan's name was at the bottom. Even though Josie had already told Dane about it, it was still unreal to see it. She clicked on his name, but there was no more information. It was blank.

"Is there another place Pierce kept his notes? He must've written down his findings."

"I was thinking the same thing. If you'll look at the date of entry, it was over six months ago—about two months before his death. And Harlan's death was only a week before Pierce's."

"Pierce had probably found his conclusions or was close by then. And since a company's bank statement was found under Harlan's body, we can conclude it had to do with missing money at our company."

"Do you know how much was missing?"

"Not the exact amount, but it was a thousand here and there for a period of several months.

And then thirty thousand dollars went missing all at once, and I think that's when Harlan believed the missing money was not some clerical error. Harlan handled the money and business end, while I talked with contractors and dealt with sales."

Josie looked up at him. "That's a *lot* of money. How come it took so long to notice?"

Dane shrugged. "I don't think it did. At first, it was a hundred here or there that the books were off. And then the amounts increased. Harlan didn't discuss the specifics with me, but normally with our accountant or the job foreman."

"He trusted you?"

Instantly, his heart picked up the pace. He wasn't a thief. "Harlan and I were close. He had no reason to doubt me."

At his sharp tone, she waved her hand downward, telling him to calm down. "I'm not accusing. Were the accountant and job foreman questioned?"

He nodded. "I think so, at least by Harlan. My partner had several closed-door meetings with both men. I can only assume they were ruled out. When Harlan was murdered and the was money found in my account, the authorities zoomed in on me."

"Okay. Byron is the foreman. And the accountant..."

"Jim Price. Price and Monroe Accounting in Dallas."

"Thanks." She jotted down the name and glanced back to the laptop. "I'm going to continue to go through more of his files. Hopefully, I'll find the name of who he was looking into. If it was the accountant or job foreman there might be something in his notes.

"Thanks." Dane walked out of the room and when he passed by Everly's door, he noticed she wasn't in sight. He stopped and looked in, not wanting to alarm Josie. He whispered, "Everly?"

Dexter wasn't in the room either. Surely, the girl wouldn't have disappeared either. He was tempted to go look for her before he alerted Josie, but that wouldn't be right. If he was her dad, he'd want to know. He stuck his head in the room. "Everly's not in her room."

Josie jumped to her feet and hurried past him. He followed on her heels out the back door. Josie hollered Everly's name.

While she checked the house, he went straight to the shed. When he opened the door, he stopped in his tracks. Everly was sitting on a plastic tub with her face in her hands and Dexter at her feet. Was she crying?

"Everly?"

She glanced up at him and quickly turned her back to him. "Go away."

He turned and yelled toward the house to Josie. "I found her." He stepped closer to the girl. "Are you okay? I was worried about you."

Slowly her chin lifted as she made eye contact. "I heard you talking about my daddy with Mom. I wish I could remember more about the man who killed him. I try to remember, but it's just the same thing over and over. Him holding my daddy underwater while he fought."

"You don't have to go back over the story again. We'll find him."

"The man looked at me. But I can't even tell you what color hair he had."

"That's not uncommon for people not to be able to recall details. Even for adults. Didn't you say you were inside the house?"

She nodded.

"That makes it even more difficult. You've been a big help."

That seemed to calm her, and she shot him a half smile.

Besides Violet, Dane had never spent much time with children. And since he'd moved out of his parents' house at an early age, he'd not even spent much time with her. Yes, he'd practically raised her with his mom drinking and his dad's absence, but after he moved out and got a place of his own, his mom asked him not to come around. Said that it upset Violet.

He had a hard time believing that. His sister had adored him. Had something changed her mind? Or had his parents made the story up? But to what end?

Either way, he intended to gain custody of her. He brought his attention back to Everly. "Hey, you've had a lot of changes in the last months. You're doing great, kiddo."

"I don't want to be the cause of anyone getting hurt."

He cocked his head at her. "You don't really believe that, do you? The only person responsible for hurting anyone is the person doing it. You're only ever, ever responsible for your own actions. Do you understand?"

She nodded. "I get it. I am eight."

"And smart as a whip." If the situation wasn't so serious, he could've laughed. To take so much burden on at such a young age was cruel.

"Everyone all right out here?" Josie stepped into the shed.

"Come on in. We were just talking."

Josie glanced from Everly to him—a strange expression on her face. "It'll be dark soon. Are you ready to go?"

"Sure." He dusted off his jeans and gave Everly a hand up from the box she was sitting on. He wished he knew what Josie was thinking. One thing was clear, she wasn't happy. Almost like she'd looked years ago when he'd disappointed her.

No matter how hard he tried, it seemed he kept letting her down?

NINE

Silence followed her as Josie settled into her chair in her living room after they returned from going to Dane's and Harlan's construction offices. To her disappointment, they had found no more evidence. On first visit to a crime scene, often an investigator could see things more clearly than a person who was familiar with the premises.

She couldn't help but feel like she'd let Dane and Everly down.

After seeing the building though, her appreciation grew for Dane and the effort he'd put into their construction business. The offices were tidy and looked professional. When they were through searching the office, they returned Nellie's car back to her home. She remembered Everly's mention of the name Nellie whom she'd overheard her dad reference.

Since Chandler was researching the foreman, she'd called Kennedy and Silas to get their expertise. They both agreed Everly needed to look at mug shots. Technically, Silas was a Texas Ranger and not on the team, but he was a good guy to have around on cases anyway. The sun set low in the sky in her living room window.

Irritation nipped at her, but she wasn't sure why. Was she jealous Dane seemed to have a way with her daughter? Hopefully not. Josie had never been petty. Everly had a close relationship with her dad, and that was probably why she seemed to draw close to Dane. The girl was only three when her mom died so she wouldn't have memories of her.

Patience was the key, but she'd never guessed how insecure or hurtful it would be that Everly hadn't trusted her enough to share the story of her father's death right off the bat. She knew better, but still she struggled to keep the feelings from surfacing.

The next morning, Josie called investigator Patty Lynch at the Liberty police station to set up an appointment. She didn't want to put pressure on Everly, but it'd be a big help if she could identify her dad's killer, and Josie had just received the call saying she could bring her in. She stepped into her room. "Honey, can I talk to you?"

"Sure." Everly scooted over on the bed.

She sat beside her daughter. "How do you feel about going down to the police station and looking at mug shots? Would that be okay? Or would it make you nervous?"

"What are mug shots?"

"When a person is arrested, the police take a photo of them."

"Oh, you mean when they turn sideways or look at the camera?" At Josie's nod, she continued. "I've seen those. Will the people in jail be able to see me?"

"No. You can sit in an office at a desk. I don't want you to confuse this with a lineup where you're in a room looking at suspects."

"Oh. Okay. I don't mind."

Poor thing. Josie could understand how she got the two confused. Many shows or movies showed the lineup. She patted her leg. "Let me know if you have any more questions."

Everly nodded. "Can Dexter go, too?"

"Hmm." The collie was a barker. That might be distracting. "You want to see if Dane wants to ride with us and he can sit in the Bronco with Dexter?"

"Okay." Her shoulders shrugged.

Several minutes later, they all rode in silence. Josie was learning that Everly's quietness did not necessarily mean something was wrong, so she let her enjoy the peaceful time.

When they grew close, Jose turned into a city park and pulled to the back of parking lot, closet to the trees. Everly hugged Dexter bye.

Dane climbed out with Dexter's leash in his

hand and looked at Josie. "I'll stay here unless you need me."

"Thanks. We'll be fine." As she drove out of the park, she noted there were only a handful of people there—two were walking their dogs and another appeared to be a mom with her two young children. The police station sat only thirty yards on the other side of the woods.

Josie and Everly walked up the steps and through the glass door. Tile floors and an open reception area greeted them. Josie had been here several times and recognized Mark behind the desk. "Good morning."

"Hi, Josie. Investigator Lynch is waiting for you in her office." He looked at Everly and then back to Josie. "Can she have a snack or something to drink? We have donuts in the break room, and I can get her a soda?"

She glanced down. "Would you like that?"

"Sure." Everly smiled.

A minute later, he came back with a soda and a chocolate donut with sprinkles. "Here you go, princess."

Everly took them and thanked him.

Josie shot him a smile and was glad they did everything possible to make children less nervous. Events like this had a way of staying with a child for the rest of their life—whether good or bad.

"Hello," Patty said when they walked into her office.

"Patty, this is Everly." Josie rested her hand on her daughter's shoulder.

Everly shook Patty's outstretched hand.

Patty kept a smile on her lips. "Your mom told me you saw a man at your house when your daddy died. Is that right?"

Everly nodded.

Josie stood off to the side to allow Patty room, but she also wanted Everly to know she was there for her. Her chest tightened at what her daughter must be feeling right now. Remembering her own childhood during and after the fire had been life changing. Although Everly witnessing her father's murder couldn't be undone, Josie hoped to offer Everly comfort and a safe place to talk.

"This seat is for you." Patty pushed a chair on wheels next to Everly. "Here's a place for your donut and soda. First, I want you to know what a brave girl you are to come in and do this for us. After I'm through explaining how this works, if you have any questions, please ask. There are no silly questions. If I ask you something and you don't know the answer, just say you don't know. Okay?"

"Okay." Everly nodded.

"When your mom called, she gave me a description of the man you saw. But I'd like to hear what happened from you. Can you tell me what you saw that day?"

"Sure." Everly's eyebrows scrunched together. "My dad and I were working outside. He mowed our lawn and then was using the weed trimmer. Daddy made me pick up my toys and Dexter's chew toys in the yard. I went inside to go to the bathroom and to get us some lemonade because it was hot outside."

Josie realized she was holding her breath and tried to relax. It was no use. Her heart hurt for the girl.

The investigator nodded. "That was helpful of you."

Everly half smiled. "I poured us some glasses, but then heard somebody yelling. I looked out the window and there was a man arguing with my daddy. I was afraid to go outside so I hid behind the door and peeked out the window."

"What did you see?" Patty coaxed her.

"The man hit my daddy and then they started fighting. My daddy got in several punches when the man tried to stab him with a knife.

"I screamed. Daddy looked at me and the man shoved my daddy into the hot tub and held him under water. Daddy fought and kicked the man in the face, but the bad man kept holding him under. Once Daddy quit moving, the man threw the weed trimmer into the water and sparks flew.

I screamed again, and the man looked at me. Then the electricity went off in the house.

"I ran out the front to my treehouse. That's when Dexter, my dog, bit the man, and he kicked my dog. Then the FedEx truck pulled up and I saw the man run behind the house. He yelled at me that if I told anyone, he would kill me. A car started up, and I didn't see him anymore."

Moisture lined Patty's eyes as she gave Everly a hug. She glanced at Josie with an *I'm sorry* look.

A tear rolled down Josie's cheek.

"You did fantastic, Everly. Now let's go back to the man and what he looked like. Can you recall how tall he was, or if he was fat or skinny?"

"I don't know how tall, but he wasn't fat or skinny."

"Good. Do you know if he was taller than your dad?"

She shrugged. "Not really."

Josie's heart went out to her as she tried to recall such an incident.

"Did he have a moustache or a beard?"

She shook her head. "I don't think so."

Josie noticed Patty used easy words such as beard instead of asking if he had facial hair. She appreciated the simple gesture. Patty had been with the police department for several years, but Josie didn't know if she had kids or a family.

"Where did Dexter bite the man?" Patty asked.

"On his arm."

"You're doing great, Everly. Now think, do you know which arm?"

Everly's eyebrows knitted. "Uh, this one." She patted her arm. "Right."

"Excellent. Okay, we're going to look through some photographs and if you see the man who was at your daddy's house, just let me know. Even if you aren't certain, let me know if any of the people look like the man. Can you do that?"

"Yeah." Everly moved closer to the desk as Patty typed a couple of things into the computer and then turned the screen for Everly to view.

Josie watched intently as Patty scrolled through several slides.

"Maybe that one." Everly pointed to a dark-haired man. Robert Latham. Forty-one years old.

Josie didn't recognize him.

"Or maybe him." This man had lighter hair and was thirty-two years old.

Patty said, "Okay…"

Josie tried not to be disappointed, but she knew it was difficult even for adults to be able to re-call details in the middle of a dangerous event. Several more minutes passed, and Everly pointed out another man.

Her daughter rubbed her eyes and sighed.

Patty patted her on the shoulder. "You're doing wonderful, Everly. Why don't we take a small break? You can finish your donut while I speak with your mom."

She stepped to the corner with Josie. "I don't want you to be disheartened. Everly is really doing great. Even if none of these are the man, we're building a base for the sketch artist. If it's all right with you, I'll set up an appointment with him later in the week."

They'd been attacked several times, and she didn't want to put off finding this jerk any longer than necessary. "Is there any way Everly can meet with him today?"

"You know we're a small department, but I'll give him a call in a minute and see what I can do. No promises, though."

"I appreciate that."

While Patty left to check on schedules, Josie went over to Everly and visited quietly. Soon Patty returned.

"He rearranged his schedule and can get to you on Thursday."

At least that was better than Friday. "Thanks."

"Do you think she can look for a few more minutes?"

"I'm sure that's fine but let me ask." Everly agreed. Thirty minutes later, they walked out of the investigator's office with a few leads. Everly had picked a total of five men she believed could be the man. One man by the name of Ronnie Hugg Josie recognized. When she looked at his file, she remembered why. He had a prior arrest for possession of cocaine with intent to sell when she'd worked for the sheriff's department. Ronnie had sold primarily to kids in junior and high schools. Josie had been the one to stake out a popular hangout close to the lake that he worked.

She tried to recall what the man with the knife had sounded like. She didn't know if he was the same or not because she'd barely talked to Ronnie. According to his file, he was six feet tall. Even though he was tall, she would've thought the knife man was taller. It wouldn't hurt to check him out.

They drove to the park and found Dane leaning against a picnic table with Dexter.

"Did he get tired of waiting?"

"You could say that." Dane shook his head in playful disgust. "Dexter was running around smelling of everything. But when he started barking at the kids on the climbing tower, I decided we were better off hiking through the trees as to not draw attention to ourselves."

Everly patted him on the head. "Oh, Dexter. You're supposed to be quiet." The collie cocked his head to the side.

Dane glanced at Josie. She was certain he was wondering if Everly identified her daddy's killer. Instead of discussing it in front of her, she held her finger up, telling him they would talk in a bit.

After they climbed in her vehicle, she asked,

"Besides Dexter taking advantage of you, did anything else happen?"

"No. I kept my eye on the traffic in front of the station but nothing suspicious."

She read between the lines that he didn't spot the silver GMC or the black Dodge. That was good that the guy hadn't followed them to the police station. "Let's go back to my place where I can do some research."

His gaze crossed to her. "Okay."

She could tell by his look that he knew she had at least one lead. It'd been years since she'd seen Dane, but it was funny that they still seemed to be able to communicate without saying words. She'd forgotten about that connection with him and missed it. In school, she'd always been a good student who stayed out of trouble and who most teachers liked. But there was that day in Mrs. Dillard's class that she and Dane had gotten in trouble for laughing during a movie and not being able to stop. The thing was they were sitting across the room from each other and still were able to converse just by reading each other's facial expressions. She looked at him, and he looked back. There was something about his eyes that made her stomach do a little flip. He'd always been a good-looking guy, even if he never realized it. She needed to be careful. They'd been high school sweethearts. Nothing more. The feelings were probably more sentimental than real since he was her first love. But with him once again running from the law, he'd not make a good family man.

She needed to keep that in mind. It was going to be hard considering how much he was risking his life to help her and Everly.

Dane sensed Josie had learned something while at the station, but he knew better than to ask in front of Everly.

Twenty minutes later, they pulled up to Josie's home. He agreed to sit with Everly while she checked out the house. There was no sign of anything out of order and they went in.

Everly had no sooner half-shut her bedroom door, before he asked, "What did you learn?"

"Not much." She pulled out her laptop and opened it up. "Everly identified five men that looked like her daddy's killer, but she wasn't certain on any of them. Do you know Ronnie Hugg?"

"The name sounds familiar. Did he play college football?"

She frowned. "No, I don't think that's the same guy. Do you mean Ron Huston?"

"Yeah, that was him. I didn't know Huston very well either, just heard his name."

As she started to type on her keyboard, she pushed a piece of paper across the table. "What about the rest of these guys?"

He glanced down at the list of names and photos and pointed. "Only this one."

"Robert Latham? Where do you know him from?"

"I didn't know his name, but he used to work at the convenience store close to our company."

"Did you or Harlan have issues with him?" Josie asked. "A disagreement? Anything that would make him want to come after Harlan?"

"No. About two years ago, he worked the early shift, and I'd stop in and buy coffee in the mornings. Then one day there was a lady behind the counter, and I never saw him again. But it's not unusual to have a high turnover rate at those kinds of places."

"Okay. Let me see what we can find on him. First, his arrest record." A minute later, she had it pulled. "DWI and vehicular manslaughter. There are a few older things on here from when he was younger. Driving under the influence and driving without a license."

Dane shook his head. "Those charges should have nothing to do with me or Harlan."

"It doesn't sound like it, but let me see who died in the accident, and I'll also check out Ronnie Hugg's family to make certain there are no connections." Her fingers paused on the keyboard as she glanced at the list again. "I'm going to look at all five of these men and see if we can find a tie-in."

At the mention of family, Dane wondered about his dad's incarceration. He'd been concentrating his efforts on the people he and Harlan both knew; he hadn't thought about anyone else. "My dad was in the Beto Unit near Tennessee Colony in Anderson County. Can you make sure none of the men served at the same time?"

"Certainly."

He glanced back to make sure Everly wasn't standing at the door. "How did Everly do? Is she okay?"

Brown eyes stared back at him before her shoulders slumped. "It's difficult for her. The investigator had Everly tell everything again she remembered about the day her daddy died."

At her pause, Dane's chest constricted. Pain radiated in her face, and her lip trembled so slightly that he wondered if he imagined it. He scooted over a chair and sat beside her. "I'm sorry, Josie." He wanted to take her into his arms to offer comfort but remembering how slow she'd been to warm up to people, he simply rested his hand on hers. "That must've been excruciating for you to endure, too. You're good with her."

A sharp laugh came from her. "I don't think so."

"What? Are you serious? You're patient with her and getting an eight-year-old child to confide in you at all is a big accomplishment."

She stared down and shrugged. "I feel like I'm

failing her at every turn. If she would've trusted me, she wouldn't have run away but told me what happened."

"You sound pathetic."

Her head jerked up. "I'm not pathetic. I don't feel sorry for myself."

"Ah, there's the old Josie." He chuckled. He'd known the crack would make her come up fighting. The truth was Josie rarely bemoaned her troubles, even when deserved. She was a tough lady that preferred to hit a problem head on. "It takes time to build trust. Don't rush it. You of all people should know that. It took me forever to get you to accept a ride in my grandma's Oldsmobile with the dented fender."

A smile tugged at her lips. "It's been forever since I've thought of that car. I know you're right." As if she just noticed his hand was still on hers, she pulled away. "I need to get back to work."

"I'd like to sit here if you don't mind."

"Make yourself comfortable."

He stayed there looking over her shoulder as she researched each person thoroughly. When Everly came out of her room, Dane prepared them all something to eat, and then he and Josie ate by her desk. After four hours of digging, nothing significant popped up.

She pushed back from her desk and stretched. "Do you think we're missing a connection?"

"Could be." She shrugged. "As the pieces come together into one place and a whole picture is developed, normally it rules people out or warrants more questions to be answered."

"Any person nagging at you? Because right now, none of the people stand out. Robert Latham is the only person I had a brief acquaintance with. The other four are strangers to me."

"But the person may not have any connection to you but may have with Harlan."

"What about Byron Ferguson, my job foreman?"

"Chandler didn't find anything concerning him. He's forty-two years old, divorced as of five years ago and he has a twenty-one-year-old son. And I checked on the partial license plate, but nothing came up belonging to your foreman. I don't mind digging deeper. Besides him being at your office, what bugs you?"

"I guess it's just that he and his friend were there and seemed to be looking for something. But what? And why now? The younger guy was talking on his cell phone to someone like he was being guided."

"Like he was on a quest for someone else?"

"Yeah, maybe." Dane ran his fingers through his hair. "He asked where he hid it. Makes me think they were searching for something that could be incriminating."

"If that's true, then it's possible something was

left by another employee or by the killer when he struck Harlan."

"Yeah." He drew a deep breath. "But I looked through the office and didn't find anything—unless Byron took something with him."

"Are you certain it was a friend with Byron?"

"Why are you asking?"

"Hold on. I saw something earlier." She looked back to her laptop. "Right here on Samantha Ferguson's social media account." She scrolled down. "Is that your guy?"

A man about twenty stood with his arm wrapped around a girl of about the same age, at what looked like a pro football game. "That looks like him. Hard to tell with him in a baseball cap, but he has the same build and age. Who is he?"

"Kyle Ferguson. The foreman's son. I couldn't find a social media account for Byron, but I looked up his ex-wife. Let me see if I can find a better picture."

Dane watched from over her shoulder. Another photo came up without the cap, showing his dark, curly hair. "Stop. That's him."

"Okay. I'll try to learn what Kyle and Byron were doing there."

"Good." They needed to make progress. "I think I need to go visit my mom and brother. Maybe the crime has to do with them."

She nodded. "The gunman and the murder of Harlan may not have anything to do with you.

But you were simply at the wrong place at the wrong time."

He got to his feet. "You don't know how many times I've told myself that. But if so, how did the money get into my account? Someone wanted the blame put on me."

"Good point. How would someone find your account number to do that?"

He shrugged. "Did I mention it showed the money was deposited *after* Harlan's death?"

"After? Wouldn't that suggest Harlan wasn't investigating the missing money then?"

"It went missing weeks before his murder. I still get monthly bank statements in the mail. Someone could steal that from my mailbox."

"Have you missed any statements?"

"Not that I know of, unless it was the last one. Of course, the envelope could've been opened and then resealed. Maybe far-fetched, but possible. Now that I think about it, I don't think they put the account number on the statement. Wait." He snapped his fingers. "Direct deposit. When I was going through the employee files, I came across the paperwork with my bank information for direct deposit. It had my account number."

"That would make sense. Most companies shred sensitive documents after the information is entered online. But maybe not smaller companies."

Dane shoved his hands into his pockets. "I

need to walk around and burn off a little energy because I tend to think better when on the move."

"I understand." She gave a big yawn and stood. "Sitting in a chair tends to exhaust me, almost like driving."

"Will you be okay while I go visit with my mom tomorrow or do I need to stay here?"

"We'll be fine." She shooed her hands at him.

"What about tonight?"

"Deputies are driving by occasionally."

"And yet no one has stopped since I've been here." Did they not notice his motorcycle in the backyard? He needed to move it out of sight. "I can sleep outside…"

Her hands went into the air. "No need to say anything more. I don't think I need protection, but I also didn't think I would need any on the camping trip. Would you like to stay here, at least until tomorrow and one of my team members is available?"

He nodded. "Yeah, I would. If I didn't, I'd never be able to sleep anyways unless I knew you and Everly were safe."

Like she said, this was temporary. As the thought came to him, he couldn't imagine leaving her safety to anyone else. For Josie to agree to let him stay meant she understood the dangers were high.

TEN

Josie checked the house once more, making certain all the doors were locked and nothing appeared out of the ordinary. On the way to the living room, she stopped at Everly's open door. The poor child must be exhausted. She was fast asleep with Dexter lying at her side. Josie wasn't certain she wanted the dog in the bed, but for now, she wasn't about to stop the practice. For several seconds she watched her daughter breathe. Emotion clogged her throat. She would protect her no matter the costs.

Hopefully, the list of suspects they'd assembled tonight would help catch the man who'd attacked them. She padded back to the couch and prepared it with a sheet and pillow for her to sleep. After she brushed her teeth, she noted the light on under her door. Dane must still be up and working. It was nice to have him working the case with her, but she wished he'd get some sleep.

She could've given him the couch, but she wanted to be closer to Everly. Silly as it was, the living room was only a few feet closer to her daughter's room than her own bedroom, but it was enough to make a difference.

The door swung open, making her jump.

"Good night." His voice sounded way too jolly for this time of night. "I want to thank you for your help. For the first time since I found my partner murdered, I feel...some hope."

She cleared her throat. "Try to get some rest. I'm sure we'll have a busy day tomorrow." Inwardly, she shook her head. She sounded like Fretful Frieda, a character in a children's book she'd had as a child. Certainly, Dane was old enough to know when to go to bed.

"I will." A smile crossed his lips. "And I didn't mean to scare you. I heard your footsteps outside my door. Thought maybe you'd heard from one of your team members."

"Not yet. I may try to contact them again. I'm going to get some sleep."

"Let me know if you learn anything. I'm going to stay awake for a while so if you hear me walking around, just know I'm keeping an eye on things."

"Okay." She headed back to the living room and heard his door shut. She hoped tomorrow would be a good day for both of them. If Dane had been framed, and she believed he was, then he needed to prove his innocence.

She clicked on the lamp next to the couch and

turned off the overhead light. Once she was settled under the sheet, she stared up at the ceiling and the swirling fan. Her legs hurt and her head slightly ached probably due to the lack of sleep and getting hit in the head by that limb. Suddenly, her mind went to the laptop she'd left plugged in on the coffee table. There was no reason it would start a fire, was there? Quietly, she climbed out from the sheet and walked to the table and shut down her computer. Logically, she knew most people left things plugged in all the time and nothing happened, but she couldn't relax until everything was safe.

Seconds later, she lay back down and turned off the lamp. With Dane in the house to help watch for intruders, she hoped to get some much-needed rest. With a fluff of her pillow, she rolled to her side and closed her eyes. Today's events went through her mind as she tried to relax. Once Pierce's murderer was behind bars, she planned to get Everly into counseling with Kennedy. There was no shame in getting help, and her team member's specialty was working with families of missing children. Surely if Kennedy could help with the trauma of missing children, she could help Everly with the death of her father. Not only for Everly, but Josie hoped Kennedy could help her with the loss of her family.

She'd never told anyone the details about the fire—nothing besides the fact that the family couldn't get out in time. How did you explain that it was your fault the fire started that killed your family? That she'd been angry her parents wouldn't let her have her best friend, Stacy, over for a sleepover. Josie had already set up the play tent in her room so she and Stacy could sleep inside while listening to some new music Stacy had downloaded. When her parents told her it wasn't a good night for company, she was mad and decided to sleep in the basement to get far away from everyone and be alone. If she hadn't been in the basement, she would've died with the rest of the family.

Or, as she preferred to believe, she could've saved them.

It was later determined the fire had started in her bedroom with an electrical cord that ran under the tent.

Looking back, she realized that had not been the healthiest decision not to seek counseling.

A door creaked and soft footsteps came out of her bedroom.

"It's just me," Dane's voice whispered to her.

"Okay," she whispered back. She was glad he was there. Ever since she'd adopted Everly, she'd constantly worried about keeping her safe and struggled to rest. Her eyes drifted shut.

Dane tried to be quiet as he stepped through the house, taking his time staring out of each window. Clouds drifted over the moon and a few stars sparkled. A gentle breeze made the limbs dance in the oak outside. The only light was near the old shed, which shone on the ground below. A frog hopped across the grass and out of sight.

His gun was in a holster shoved into the back of his waistband just in case there was trouble. Josie was competent at protecting her daughter, he had no doubt. But even the best law officer, or in her case former law officer, could be overtaken if the conditions were just right. With the list of suspects, he prayed he could turn himself in once the sheriff had returned.

Trust had never come easy, and he hoped he wasn't wrong in putting his faith in Josie. Her watching as he was arrested was scorched into his memory—the shiny eyes, the corner of her lips drawn downward. Not only did she appear sad, but also resigned. Like she was doing what she must. If she'd just come to his defense, maybe the police would've believed him—or at least asked more questions about Keaton. With Keaton being the DA's son, it had been easy to accept his word, and pin the theft on Dane.

They had gone out for months, and he remembered being blown away that she accepted his date when other kids pulled away from him or ignored him. But Josie had been different. Beautiful and athletic. She had been one of the few who talked with him. If it hadn't been for her living a half mile from him, he never would've had the chance. He had been a goofy kid, but she'd given him confidence.

Her grandpa didn't seem to have much money, but that didn't stop her from being popular by his standards.

Protectiveness consumed him at the thought of the same man who killed Harlan, targeting her and her daughter. Besides Violet, there wasn't anyone in his life he cared so much about.

Clank.

The noise came somewhere from outside. He stiffened as he peered through the window. A leaf blew across the drive, but there were no other activities nor shadows. It sounded like it came from the right of his vantage point, so he hurried back to his bedroom. He intended to look out the window, but when he came through the door, movement came from the closet.

He reached back for his gun, and something hard came down on his head. Fireflies danced in the air.

And then he was stumbling, trying to keep his footing. Josie and Everly were vulnerable sleeping.

He tried to put his hands out to break the fall, but his arms collapsed as he hit the floor. Everything went black.

Josie's brain wrestled in a fog of memories. Her childhood home filled with breath-stealing smoke.

Family members' shouts reverberated from the top floor.

Her dad's voice echoed through the dark home, "Fire! Get out!"

"Audrey!" her mom called. "Where are you?"

Footsteps pounded across the floor above her. Josie fumbled out of the bed in the basement and hurried up the stairs. The smoke grew thicker the higher she climbed. Dizziness descended on her as she reached the top. When she swung the door open, flames whooshed in front of her. She yelled, "Mom!"

The dark haze blinded her, but flickers from the flames illuminated her dad's silhouette. "Josie. Go back downstairs and climb out the window."

"What about Audrey?"

"I'll get your sister. Go now! Get out of the house and don't come back in." His shout spurred her into action as she sprinted down the dark stairs. She hacked, her lungs begging for air.

The cough racked her body and her chest burned.

"Mom!" The child's voice called from far away.

The word demanded her attention, and Josie shot straight up on the couch. Barking came from the other room.

Everly!

"Get down on the floor. I'm coming for you." Smoke burned her eyes, making it difficult to see.

She'd scarcely made it to her feet when the blazing ceiling fell on her, and she was barely able to block it to keep from taking the brunt of it. Burning debris dropped like rain all around her.

More barking came from Everly's room. The fire would spread slower if there was no oxygen.

"Shut the door, Everly."

But it was too late.

"Help me." Her daughter's voice came from the hallway.

"Get down on the floor. I'm coming to you." Heat blocked her path, but she had to save her daughter. She turned and ran toward the kitchen and away from Everly. The fire had not engulfed this part of the house yet. Before running out the back door, she hollered one last time. "Go back in your room and shut the door. Trust me."

Moving faster than she believed possible, she sprinted barefoot down the porch and around the side of the house to Everly's room. In her mind, she prepared to break out the window since she knew it was locked, but the girl had the pane open. Dexter barked.

Josie held out her hands. "Come here."

Everly leaped into her arms, Dexter right behind her. The girl coughed and gagged, and Josie carried her away from the flames. With all of her might, she tried not to break down, flooded with relief, but it was no use. Her limbs shook uncontrollably. "Are you hurt? Did you get burned?"

"I'm okay."

Despite her words, tears ran down her daughter's face; no doubt, scared to death. Dexter continued to bark and circle them with excitement as the flames reached high into the sky. Small explosions mixed with whooshing, and pops filled the void.

"Mom, where's Dane?"

She inhaled a sharp intake of breath. She'd been so concerned with saving Everly, she'd forgotten about him. As she ran around the backside of the house, an explosion rocked the ground. As if danger was everywhere and closing in, it suddenly hit her, someone must have started the fire.

That person might still be close by.

"Everly." She turned. "Get inside my Bronco and lock the doors. Take Dexter with you."

While her daughter ran barefoot in her gown toward the garage, déjà vu swept over her. She couldn't lose another person in a fire. The last she'd seen of Dane he was walking through the house trying to protect her and Everly.

She prayed he wasn't in the home, but his motorcycle was still in the driveway. She ran toward the flames. *Please, Lord, help him be okay.*

ELEVEN

A massive ache pounded through Dane's head and stampeded back and forth like a jackhammer. His lungs burned, making it impossible to breathe, and the heat was unbearable. It took a millisecond for the cobwebs to clear and for him to realize something was wrong.

Deadly wrong.

Deafening pops and a constant sizzling encompassed him. Even the wooden floor felt warm to his cheek. He rolled over to see the ceiling above him ablaze while pieces of sheetrock crashed to the floor.

Josie and Everly. He had to get to them.

He climbed to his feet, making the heat increase, and dizziness swirled through him. He stumbled toward the door. Orange flames kicked up all around, singeing the side of his jeans. When he opened the door, a raging inferno whooshed through the opening. He couldn't exit this way and shoved the door closed. He'd have to go around the side of the house to get them out.

As he turned and staggered back toward the window, his world spun. No matter how much he attempted to take a breath, his lungs wouldn't fill. It felt like he was breathing through a coffee straw.

Over the crackling of the flames, a faint voice called his name.

Josie? "In here." As soon as the words were out, a burning board fell from above and hit him in the shoulder, knocking him down. He still couldn't breathe.

Fear like he'd never felt before assaulted him. He wasn't going to survive. Not this time.

What would happen to Violet? And Josie and Everly? Had the killer already found them?

He had to get out of there. Shoving his pain aside, he attempted to get to his feet. But it was no use. The lack of oxygen zapped his energy.

"Dane." Josie's voice called again.

He opened his mouth to answer but gagged and coughed instead. *Stay out. Don't try to save me.* He didn't know if he said the words out loud, but he didn't want her to die.

Please, God, if You get me out of here alive, I will try to do better. I'll try my hardest to help Josie, Everly, and Violet. Just let me live.

Somewhere in the distance, sirens wailed. There was no way Dane could survive by the time they reached her house. After running back to the shed, Josie found a box of bed sheets and grabbed a stack. A blanket would be better, but there was no time to search. She hurried to the water spigot and held the fabric underneath, then sprinted back to the house. A quick glance showed Everly's face plastered against the driver's side window of her Bronco watching her.

Please, let Dane be okay. She yelled, "Watch out. I'm going to break the window."

She prayed he was still in her bedroom. Using a bulky decorative rock from her landscaping, she threw it with all of her might. The stone went straight through, and left a decent hole in the pane, but not large enough for her to crawl through. Wrapping the sheet around her elbow and arm for protection, she finished knocking out the pane and climbed through.

Instantly a wall of heat suffocated her, and she pulled the wet sheet over her core. "Dane. Where are you?"

She dropped to the floor that was littered with tiny fires. Heat burned her eyes, forcing her to temporarily close them. Not being able to see, she felt around with her hand. Was the door to the bedroom open? She couldn't remember. At this point, it didn't matter. Her bed was to her right and the bathroom on her left. She hadn't crawled a couple of feet when her hand touched something firm—his shoulder. "Dane. Are you okay?"

He groaned, and his hand reached out and touched her cheek. "Josie."

"Here. Cover up with this. Help is on the way, but we need to get you out of here. Can you crawl to the window?"

His voice was gravelly. "Save yourself. Get out."

"Not without you."

He got on his knees and elbows, while she helped keep the damp sheet around him. As she assisted him, her sheet got tangled under her knees and fell to the floor. It didn't take long to make it to the window, and Dane grabbed the frame and pulled himself up, his muscles trembling from the effort.

As smoke was sucked from the window, blackness descended on them. Something exploded—engulfing them in a heat cloud.

"Come on. Let's get you out of here." But Dane slumped back to the floor.

The flames grew larger. "Out the window. I can't pick you up."

He climbed to his knees and then to his feet, leaning against the window. With her help, he was able to fall and roll out of the window frame and onto the ground. More hissing and popping sounded. The house was old and used propane for heat. The tank sat on the other side of the building, and she wondered how much longer it would be until it exploded.

Sitting on the window frame, she jumped feet first and landed beside Dane. They stumbled across the yard as the sirens grew louder.

Boom! The ground shook as a huge fireball ballooned across the land.

Seconds later and neither of them would've made it.

Josie watched as the fire ravaged her house. "This was too close. We must catch whoever is targeting us."

Dane leaned up on his elbows, his face and clothes a dark mask of soot. He fought to get to his feet. "I've got to get out of here."

"Dane, no..."

Regret lined his face. His gaze searched hers before he leaned forward and gave her a peck on her cheek. "Thanks for helping me out. I owe you." And then he took off between the outbuildings and disappeared into the darkness.

Josie made her way over to her Bronco, as the last of the fire trucks stopped in her drive. Multiple emergency vehicles arrived, including Deputy Hattie Perkins's from the sheriff's department.

As Everly eagerly climbed out of the SUV, Josie wrapped her arms around her, her knees still shaking. She didn't trust her voice and held her daughter for several moments.

"Is there anyone still inside?" a tall fireman asked.

"No. Everyone made it out." Had she really gotten them all out? The feeling like someone could still be in there caused her chest to constrict, but she knew it was just the three of them.

"Are you certain?"

"Yes, sir. Even our collie is out safely."

"Okay. Stay back."

Deputy Perkins walked up but waited for the fireman to leave before she drew close. Concerned eyes examined her. "Are you okay, Josie?"

"Scared, but I wasn't injured."

"Let's check your oxygen level just in case." A paramedic put a reader on her finger. "Eighty-nine. Let's get you on oxygen and check the rest of your vitals."

As Josie sat in the back of the ambulance, she watched as the same paramedic checked out Everly. Thankfully, her daughter had suffered no harm. Deputy Perkins decided to wait to ask more questions. She was glad, considering she was wearing the oxygen mask.

Josie glanced to the area behind the shed where Dane had disappeared. As quick as the kiss had been, her cheek still tingled from the brush of his lips and the prick of his beard—not a bad thing.

The peck had been a simple gesture of appreciation. Right? Because she wasn't looking for anything more. She had her hands full with Everly and didn't need to even consider a relationship, especially while he was running from the law.

Where was he? Had he kept running or was he close by watching the scene? Her gut told her he was close.

But did she really know him that well anymore to have a sixth sense? Surely not. He couldn't keep running. It only made him look guiltier. If only he would trust the system.

Her attention returned to the home as the firemen got the blaze under control. The house would be a total loss. Thankfully, she had renter's insurance. Fifteen minutes later, she was off the oxygen and felt much better. As she walked around the perimeter of what used to be her home, Deputy Perkins caught back up with her.

"Tell me what happened, Josie."

She sighed. "I'm not certain where to begin. I told you about Everly and me being attacked at our vacation cabin."

The deputy nodded.

"I was going through some of Everly's dad's things—his laptop that was stored in boxes in my garage. I didn't even realize I had it with me until yesterday. I woke to the house being filled with smoke."

For several seconds, the woman stared at Josie. "Tel me about your involvement with Dane Haggerty."

Her heart dropped. She couldn't and wouldn't lie. But what if he was right and someone had framed him and the law didn't believe it? She had to trust in the justice system. *That's easy for you to say.* His words echoed in her mind. "How did you know about Dane?"

Perkins shrugged with a slight smile. "I didn't know for sure. But that looks like his motorcycle over there." She jerked her head.

Oh no. And Josie had fallen for the leading question. "Dane believes the man who is after Everly and me is also the man who set him up. Pierce Browning, Everly's dad, had been hired to investigate Harlan and Dane's construction company. For the record, I came to that conclusion on my own, too."

This time Perkins kept her expression unreadable. "You realize that could mean Dane could've had reason to kill Browning, too."

"I do." Josie nodded. "But if that's so, why hasn't he left the area? Why remain close?"

"You know as well as I do that criminals don't always make the smartest moves. Having family or friends in the area is enough for them to stay with what's familiar."

Violet. His sister immediately came to Josie's mind. "Hattie, you know I would never break the law or hide a fugitive."

"Unless…"

She rubbed a hand across the back of her neck.

If Dane was innocent, he needed her this time. She'd turned him in before, and now she realized she *could've* been wrong. It was at least a possibility. "Unless there was a really good reason. I don't take the law lightly."

"I won't lie to the sheriff. He needs to know." The deputy's stern expression told her there was no room for discussion.

"And I wouldn't ask you to."

Hattie pursed her lips and nodded. "Good."

After the deputy walked away, Josie considered what she'd just done. It was one thing to believe in somebody, but another to put her faith in them. Her gaze went to Everly. Not only was her own reputation at stake, but if she was wrong, it could affect her daughter's future, too.

An hour later, all emergency responders were gone except for the deputy—Hattie had agreed to see her to a hotel in town. Since her Bronco had been left unscathed, Josie climbed into the driver's seat and looked over to where Everly sat in the passenger seat fast asleep. Her daughter's eyes fluttered open as soon as Josie shut the door.

"Sorry. I didn't mean to wake you."

"I wasn't sleeping well anyway. Where will we live now?"

Josie tried to display confidence. "Home is wherever family is. It's not a building. As long as we're together, we'll be fine."

Everly didn't reply, and she hoped that was

because her answer satisfied her. The truth was, Josie had never invested much in a house, or put down deep roots, because she understood too well how fast a home could vanish. And family.

"I totally agree," a male voice said from the back seat.

Josie let out a yelp. "Dane Haggerty. You scared me half to death."

"There were too many people milling around. I knew you couldn't stay here for the night, and I thought we should get on the same page."

She glanced at him in her rearview mirror as she came to a stop at the end of her driveway.

He asked, "Where are you going?"

"To a hotel. I'm figuring Liberty Inn and Suites. Hattie is planning to be with us. That's her vehicle." Josie pointed to the deputy's SUV that just pulled out. I think she's waiting on me."

"It's good you're staying with her. That makes me feel better." He leaned forward and grimaced. "I'll call you in the morning."

Before she had time to ask anything, he exited the vehicle and moved along the fence row until he disappeared into the shadows. She noticed he hunched forward in pain, making her wonder about the extent of his injuries from the fire.

As she pulled onto the rock road, Josie looked for Dane and disappointment crashed into her when she didn't see him, leaving her with the dawning realization he was becoming important to her again.

No matter what she'd done to protect her heart, Dane had a way of breaking through the strongest of armor.

TWELVE

From the cover of a lilac bush, Dane watched Josie's Bronco pull out of the drive until it topped the hill, disappearing from sight. Pierce Browning's laptop was in the house and no longer useful in proving Pierce had been hired by Harlan.

Should he give up and turn himself in? Maybe Josie was right, and he should trust law enforcement to do their job. But the looks on the faces of the DA, the judge, and the few other people in the courtroom were still ingrained in his memory. They all believed him guilty. And then his classmates and neighbors treated him differently after he'd gotten out of juvenile detention. He'd graduated high school from there.

As he climbed to his feet, his back burned, his shirt sticking to the wound. With each move, the cloth stuck, and instant pain felt like a knife stabbing an open wound. No doubt, he needed medical care. But if he sought help, it'd be the same as turning himself in.

Josie and Everly needed his help more. The

quicker he found the guy who was targeting them, the better. The fire must've been started by him. Where did he go? Had he stayed around to watch his handiwork? Was he sending a message again, or had he really wanted to kill them? Or did he just want to destroy the laptop and anything else in those files?

So many questions and not enough answers.

As he surveyed his surroundings, his gaze stopped on the garage. Drawing his gun, he moved down the driveway, careful to stay in the shadows as much as possible. He stepped into the open garage and then the storage room at the back. A quick look produced nothing.

The man must have started the fire and left. But why not stay and act like a good neighbor or passerby? Because Everly could still identify him.

His motorcycle was still there. Thankfully, the machine had not been consumed by the fire. As he threw his leg over the seat, his back cramped in rebellion. He waited for the pain to subside before starting the motor. Cobwebs filled his mind from being only semiconscious due to the smoke—a terrible headache his reward.

Even as the idling engine rumbled, his head felt like it would explode. After he left Josie's place, he rode by the Liberty Inn and Suites. Josie and Everly were climbing the stairs to the second floor, the deputy behind them.

Now that he knew she was okay, he headed out of town to get ready for his next stop. The stakes were getting more dangerous, and he intended to do everything in his power to find out who was behind the attacks. He had the feeling the person may be closer to him than he'd first believed.

Dane knocked on the door as early morning light came over the horizon. The overgrown yard looked like it hadn't been mowed all year. Sadness hit hard. *Honor thy father and mother.* It was such a challenging commandment for him, even though he knew it was the right thing to do.

The door swung open.

Shock was the best word to describe his reaction. His mother was hunched over, and her hair had thinned and grayed. He almost didn't recognize her. "Mom."

She squinted. "Dane. Is that you?" Her voice came out weak and shaky.

"Yes, Mama. It's me." He hoped she hadn't been drinking being it was early in the morning. "Can I come in?"

"Of course. Of course." She stepped back.

The smell of cigarette smoke and something burning assaulted him as he entered the living room. Trash and junk were piled up on almost every surface in the living space. Even her old recliner was full of yarn and crochet needles. "Is something burning?"

She waved her hand. "My peas and carrots ran out of water and scorched the pan last night. I don't have no money."

"I didn't come for money." He held his breath for her to say she'd heard about the warrant for his arrest, but she didn't continue.

"Have a seat." She indicated the couch.

"No, thanks. While I'm here, I figured I might lend you a hand." He smiled and stepped into the kitchen. Dishes were stacked in the sink, and he went about transferring them to the counter. After he rinsed the sink, he ran water and squeezed in a good amount of dishwashing liquid.

His mom cleared a place at her table and sat. "What do I owe this visit to?"

He glanced at her. "I wanted to check on Violet."

"Violet?" Her voice dropped. "The court took your sister away."

"I'm sure there was an investigation. When did it start?"

"Over a year ago. They threatened to take Violet away if I didn't take parenting classes and get a job. I had been working at the diner for over thirteen years, and then they let me go."

The Greasy Spoon had fired her over two years ago for showing up intoxicated. They'd even given her time off at a rehabilitation center to help—something small businesses couldn't always afford. But his mom had not stayed sober.

After he washed several glasses and plates, he went for the bowls and larger spoons. His mom appeared frailer than he'd believed possible.

He turned to her. "I'm sorry, Mom. Is there anything I can do?"

"For Violet? No. She's gone." She rubbed her forehead. "And maybe it's for the best. Teachers and other people tended to get involved. I just couldn't be a good mom anymore. Not after you and Randy."

Dane held his tongue. His dad had been in and out of trouble, including jail, for most of Dane's life. And his dad used Randy to help steal things in stores. The first time Dane had witnessed it, he couldn't have been more than five, and Randy was about seven. His dad had gone into a jewelry store and told the clerk he wanted to buy a bracelet for his wife for her birthday. Dane remembered being surprised because he didn't realize it was her birthday. But he was also excited, believing she'd be getting a nice present. As soon as the lady had a group of bracelets displayed on the counter, Randy ran inside the store and grabbed a carousel of earrings at the end of an aisle. The whole thing crashed to the floor. The clerk told his dad to hold on, and when she hurried across the store to stop Randy, his dad stuffed several bracelets into his pockets.

They hurried to the car and then pawned the pieces on the way home.

Randy didn't have a chance to stay out of trouble as a kid. Dane didn't have much to do with his brother, but the last he'd heard, Randy was doing time in county jail.

After a load of dishes was drying, he continued to put items away and clean the kitchen.

"Why are you here? You haven't been by in a couple of years."

Did she not remember asking him not to come by? That seeing him made Violet act out. Like he was to blame. "I've got a few questions for you if you have time."

"Honey, I don't hardly get out or talk to anyone besides Alma and Stanley Hastings. They pick up food for me at the store or take me to my doctor appointments if needed. I don't have no money if that's your game."

"No game, Mom." Guilt descended on him with her words. Even though she'd asked him to not come by anymore, he should've argued or made more of an effort. "I don't know how to ask this."

"Just be honest like we've taught you."

He wasn't going to take the bait on that opening. "Did Dad have any enemies? Any that would come after our family?"

Her eyebrows furrowed. "Most people liked your father, although I'm sure there may be a few who felt otherwise. That's normal."

"Mom, he went to jail for stealing. That's bound to upset the ones he stole from."

"I'll not have you speaking ill of the dead."

He sighed and ran his hand through his hair. "I'm not trying to. I promise. I just need to know if there is anyone who may have been mad enough to target our family."

"Is someone bothering you, Dane?"

"Yeah." He grabbed the cereal boxes from the table and put them in the cabinet.

"I'd rather you leave those on the table. It makes it easier for me."

"Sorry." He put them back where he found them.

"There were a few people who didn't get along with your father. Joe Tonelli and Demarcus Howard are the worst."

"I remember them. Joe claimed Dad owed him money for work done on his old Chevy pickup, and Demarcus got into it with him over some tools that went missing when Dad did some work for him."

She nodded. "That's right. Joe rebuilt an alternator, but your dad said it didn't fix the problem, and he wasn't going to pay for it. And then he helped Demarcus combine during wheat harvest, and then the man said Tyrus stole his post-hole digger and air compressor from his shop. Your daddy had no use for those things and wouldn't have taken them."

He also had no use for diamond bracelets, but that hadn't stopped him from pawning them. "Is there anyone else that might have it in for him or our family? Maybe someone from jail?"

"Not that I can remember. He never talked much about people from those times. You know, Dane, he had his problems, but Tyrus was a good man. What's this all about?" The back door opened as she was speaking. "Are you in some kind of trouble?"

Randy walked into the room. His face lit up into a greasy smile. "Yeah, he's in trouble," his brother busted out. "Ain't that right, little brother? Running from the law. Didn't think you had it in you."

Dane had thought Randy was still serving time, but evidently he'd been released early. "Been a while, Randy."

"Mama, you know your darling Dane has a warrant for his arrest for murder?"

Her mouth dropped open and concerned etched her forehead. "For what?"

"Come on, Randy." His older brother had called him "darling Dane" for as long as he could remember, and it still grated on his nerves. He turned his attention back to their mom. "There's nothing to worry about."

His brother grabbed a beer from the refrigerator and took a big swig. Oily hair swung to his shoulders and his T-shirt was wrinkled and had a crude picture of a woman complete with a nasty saying printed across the front. "I knew you wasn't the goody-two-shoe like you thought."

Dane didn't bother with a response, although he could feel the heat rise to his cheeks. Maybe it was no one that had known their dad causing him trouble, but Randy. Did he dare ask the question? Could it be his own brother who framed him?

His stomach turned. That would be too much for even Randy.

Dane had always been a little afraid of his older brother. Maybe it was that way with a lot of siblings, but Randy took trouble to a new level. "Was this your doing?"

Randy's lips slowly turned upward. "What? That I killed somebody?" He let out a boisterous laugh. "Not hardly. Although, I could if I wanted to, and I can guarantee I wouldn't get caught. If you want me to testify for you, lil' bro, just give me the word. I have no doubt you've never hurt anyone in your life. You ain't that tough."

Dane was about to get into it with Randy. He sure wasn't going to argue that killing someone made you tough.

Worry lines formed across his mom's forehead, and he turned his attention back to her. "Mom don't be concerned. I didn't do anything wrong. I'll check on you later."

Randy dropped to the sofa, his beer sloshing to the carpet, and he watched Dane.

He gave his mom a kiss on the cheek and left

without acknowledging Randy. As he strode out the door, he wanted to tell his brother to lay off and quit upsetting their mom. But it'd do no good. Randy would welcome a confrontation.

As he took off on his motorcycle, the wind blew through his hair. Could his brother have set him up? But why? What would be the purpose? They had never been close, but they weren't enemies, not enough to lead to killing two people.

When he was several miles away from his mom's place, he pulled over at a roadside park and killed the engine. He called Josie.

"Hello."

"I have another person I'd like you to investigate if you can."

"Okay, Grandpa. Let me step out." Her voice was barely more than a whisper.

"Is the deputy close by?"

"Yeah."

It felt like a knife went into his chest. "I don't want you to lie for me, Josie. I'll make this quick. Randy Haggerty. I thought he was in prison, but he's not."

Several seconds of silence crawled by. "I can do that. I hope you're wrong, Dane."

"Me too. Can we meet so we can talk freely? How about at the old Tatum drive-in on Preston Bend."

Several seconds of silence went by. The drive-in was already closed when he and Josie started dating, but they would sometimes meet to talk there. After a few meetings, it became their place.

"I'll be there at nine o'clock tonight. Everly is still asleep. Technically, Hattie is off duty right now and said she could watch Everly if I needed to get a couple of things done. She'll be back on duty this afternoon."

"Okay. I'll see you there."

"Oh, one more thing. Do you know anyone who drives a black Ford Raptor?"

He thought for a moment. "No. Why?"

"One has driven by the hotel several times, but I wasn't able to see the license plate."

That didn't sound good. And if she left to meet him, whoever was in the Raptor might target her. "Josie, be careful."

After they disconnected, he stared at the phone. He was starting to care for her again. A lot. Just as things were becoming more dangerous.

Josie arrived at the drive-in fifteen minutes early, and Dane's motorcycle was already parked between a grove of trees and what was left of the concession stand. She pulled her Bronco next to him and killed the engine.

He opened her door for her. "You're early."

"So are you." She stepped out onto the green, overgrown grass. Even though it had been a hot day, a welcome breeze blew across the open area, reminding her of the summer nights when they used to come here.

Without thought she moved to the old metal picnic table where they used to talk for hours. She sat in her normal place on top of the table and rested her feet on the bench seat.

He stood in front of her and glanced down. "Did you learn anything more?"

"Several things. Chandler paid a visit to Byron to find out why he and his son were at the office."

"Yeah." Hope sounded in his voice. "Tell me you learned something helpful."

"It looks like nothing but dead ends. A few days after the murder, Byron stopped by to grab his personal belongings, and Kyle and his girl-friend came with him. While Byron was loading up his things, Kyle and his girlfriend were look-ing at the murder scene and the offices. His girl-friend accidentally left her purse or wallet there that contained her identity. Being that her par-ents didn't want her dating Kyle and her dad is police officer in Pine Hollow, she was afraid her parents would find out if investigators searched the premises. Kyle agreed to grab the wallet and give it back."

He held his hands out to his side. "It took them months to figure that out?"

"The two were no longer talking, and it took her that long to remember where she'd left it. Chandler believed them."

Dane rubbed the back of his neck. "I always liked Byron, so I suppose I should be relieved. Anything else?"

"Chandler also checked out Jim Price, the accountant. He seems clean with no red flags. I researched your brother. Randy was paroled over two months ago. I didn't find any connections to Pierce or anyone who worked with you, including Harlan."

Stormy eyes stared back at her. She couldn't tell what he was thinking, but emotions swirled. What must it be like not to trust your own family?

"What about my dad?"

She shook her head. "I'm sorry. There's nothing there either. There were no connections to prisoners in Tennessee Colony." She shrugged. "We can keep looking, but my gut says Harlan's and Pierce's murders had nothing to do with either Randy or your dad."

"I guess that's good." He looked up at the sky. "It's beautiful tonight."

The sudden change of subject surprised her. She leaned back and put her hands on the table and gazed at the sky. "The moon and stars are so bright."

Dane was silent for a few seconds, and then he sat beside her. "Reminds me of when we used to come here. I missed those days—the long talks… and stuff."

The stuff was what she didn't want to think about right now. They'd been young and in love; besides talking, they'd come here to hold hands and kiss. Once, Dane had brought a blanket so they could watch airplanes and occasionally see a shooting star. Their budding romance hadn't happened over night, but rather they'd been friends at first. He'd lived with his grandma when Josie met him, but he confided he'd lived with neighbors before then.

Even though Josie had lost her family to the fire, she'd been proud to be part of the Hunt clan. Her dad had been a supervisor at a factory, and her mom had stayed home with her and Audrey until they started school. Then she went to work for the rural water company. Nothing grand, but her parents were well thought of in the community and provided a stable homelife.

"Dane, you've done good."

Even though she wasn't looking at him, she could feel him studying her. "What's that supposed to mean?"

She turned to him then. "In business. In life."

He chuckled. "You're kidding me, right? I've been accused of murdering my business partner and best friend."

"I know it sounds silly. But I'm proud of you. Harlan believed in you. Your parents...had a difficult time."

"That's putting it lightly. Dad was a thief and Mom was an alcoholic."

Her chest constricted. "But yet you managed to help start and run a successful business."

He glanced away and gazed back at the stars. "It's more than that. Harlan introduced me to God. I realized no matter the struggles my family had, I had choices. I could choose a different path. When I started going to worship services, I also realized everyone has problems. Even the people that seem to have their life together." He turned back to her. "I was younger when I went to church with you. I didn't quite get it. I mainly went to be around you, so when you turned me in, I was ready to give up."

"I'm sorry about that." Rarely did Josie apologize. Normally the sentiment tasted bitter, but not this time. "I should've believed in you."

"What changed your mind?"

She shrugged. "Just you. You kept telling me Keaton gave you the keys and you didn't know the car belonged to the principal. In my mind, that was unbelievable."

His eyes searched her face before he wrapped his arms around her.

She started to pull away because she didn't want to give him the wrong idea. Didn't want him to think she was interested in anything more than helping put away whoever was targeting them and clear his name. But as he held her tight, she couldn't make herself let go.

"Thank you, Josie. You don't know what it means to have your support." He released her and climbed back to his feet. "We need to find the real killer."

Instantly she missed his warmth. She cleared her throat. "You're right. Who would have something to gain?"

He shoved his hands into his pockets. "I don't know. I've gone over this a hundred times. It has to be the money. I think we should visit Layla."

"Harlan's wife?"

"Yeah.

Headlights shone along the road and then a vehicle pulled into the abandoned drive-in. Josie slid her gun from the holster and then placed it against her leg. Dane moved closer to her and pulled the bill of his ballcap further down as a squad car pulled up.

The car stopped in front of them and then an unfamiliar officer stepped out.

Josie's heart thumped in her chest. If the lady recognized Dane, he would be arrested.

"Can I ask what you two are doing out here? This is private property."

Dane eased into the shadows of the concession stand.

"Hello, officer." Josie let out a friendly laugh. "This is a little embarrassing. My high school sweetheart and I used to come here years ago. We reunited a few days ago and decided it'd be a good place to talk."

The officer shined a flashlight on Josie's face. Josie was careful to keep her gun out of view. It'd be hard to explain why she had it on her. Her mouth went dry, and her stomach rolled as the officer shined the light on Dane.

"Okay." She clicked the light off. "The owner has listed this place for sale, and he calls in to complain when someone trespasses—there's been vandals recently. You two need to move along."

"Yes, ma'am," Dane said.

The officer glanced from Dane back to Josie. "Just to give you two a piece of advice, find somewhere else to *talk*."

Awkwardness hung in the air as they watched her pull out until her taillights disappeared over the hill.

Josie released a high sigh of relief. "That was a little too close."

"You're not kidding." He looked back the way the officer had disappeared. "I'm going the other way. I don't want to take a chance of crossing paths again."

"I'll see you in the morning. I'm praying things go well when we visit Layla." The seriousness of the situation weighed heavy on her. The only thing she knew for certain was they were running out of leads and were no closer to learning who was trying to kill them. How many more times could they be attacked and come out alive? She prayed they didn't find out.

THIRTEEN

Josie took a deep breath and knocked on Layla's door.

The gorgeous stone home was trimmed in cedar and had bulky porch posts. A wide, winding stone walk accented the colorful landscaping. She glanced over her shoulder at Dane, but he was no longer in sight. He must be down in the seat.

A banging sounded from inside the house and then she watched through the glass panes of the door a pretty lady walk into the foyer. The slender woman with fiery red hair wore soft makeup that gave her a flawless look. The dark complexion shouted either she was outside a lot or suntanned at a facility. Josie figured the latter.

"May I help you?"

She smiled and held out her hand. "Yes, ma'am. I'm Josie Hunt and I'd like to ask you some questions about your husband."

The woman gave her hand a quick shake. "I've

already talked with the police. I have nothing more to say."

"Oh, no, ma'am, I'm not with the police. I'm an investigator with Bring the Children Home Project." She smiled. One mention of the organization that helped find missing kids brought down most people's defenses. Who could be rude to a person who helped reunite children with their families? Josie wasn't above using this tactic to get her foot in the door.

The woman's smile waned a bit. "Come on in. Although I'm not certain how I can help. Is there a missing child?"

"No." Josie followed her inside the entryway and cool air hit her. Tall ceilings made the home feel even larger. A huge stairway led to the second story. Plants and flowers sat along the wall, giving the place a welcoming feel. She followed the woman into a cozy room with all white furniture and bright floral pillows.

Somehow Dane's description of Harlan as down to earth didn't quite match the grand house or his exquisite wife.

"Can I get you something to drink? Lemonade? Bottled water?"

"No, thank you. First, let me offer my condolences. I can only imagine what you are going through." The woman's bright-colored shirt and teal leggings were a far cry from mourning clothes, but some people didn't tend to hold to such traditions anymore. "I'd like to know if there is anything you can tell me about Harlan before his death. Like if he was distracted."

The woman's green eyes stared straight at her. "Harlan was always distracted with work. He lived and breathed the construction business. Work is what made him the happiest, which is why it breaks my heart his partner took advantage by stealing from him. A tragic case of betrayal."

The words annoyed Josie, but they also sounded rehearsed. *A tragic case of betrayal.* Had she read that line in a book somewhere? "Yes, of course, that would be tragic. But I'm not certain Dane Haggerty is the man who killed your husband. Did Harlan keep records or documents here? I've looked at the office, but it seems some paperwork may be missing."

Layla stiffened, her face paling. "Well, you're wrong. It's obvious he killed my Harlan. Dane Haggerty is a greedy low-life varmint that couldn't wait to get his hands on my husband's business. Harlan was considering selling his half to Dane, but Haggerty was too impatient and killed Harlan with his granddaddy's hay hook."

Josie inwardly took a deep breath and gave the woman some latitude because she'd lost her husband. Dane had complained how people easily wrote him off. "But if he killed Harlan with the hay hook, why didn't he take it with him? Surely, no killer would be that ignorant."

Layla got to her feet. "He most certainly was that dumb. Harlan complained about his incompetence all the time. Why that man ever took pity on that scum I'll never understand."

A door shut somewhere in the back of the house, and Josie turned toward the sound. When she looked back to the widow, their gazes met.

"Just the AC coming on. Sometimes it causes a door to close." The woman waved her hand, dismissing the noise.

"I'm sorry for your loss, Mrs. Schmidt. I didn't mean to upset you." She asked again, "Did Harlan bring paperwork home?"

"No, he didn't." Layla's gaze wouldn't meet Josie's. "Is there something in particular you were searching for?"

"Honestly, anything that could give me insight as to why someone killed Harlan. The authorities have the bank statement that was discovered at the scene, but the previous statements appear to be missing." Financial information could easily be subpoenaed at the bank, but Josie wanted to get the widow's reaction.

Layla tugged at her collar irritably. "I understood Haggerty had the stolen money in his account. If you truly care about justice, tell the man to return the money and turn himself in. I won't be able to sleep well until my husband's killer is behind bars."

Josie smiled. "I understand. There seems to be a question of why he deposited the money in his account *after* Harlan's death. Do you know why your husband hired a PI?"

"I have no idea what you're talking about."

"Harlan hired Pierce Browning and then the investigator was killed."

Layla shook her head, but her eyes displayed doubt.

"Seems too coincidental that he was killed right after Harlan was murdered." Josie paused to see if she would reply, but Layla simply stared. "If you think of anything else, would you please give me a call?" She withdrew a business card from her purse and held it out.

The woman snatched it away from her. "I won't. And it sounds like Dane must've killed two people."

"I'll see myself out." But as Josie walked toward the front door, Layla stayed on her heels.

"If Dane wasn't guilty, why did he run? Innocent people don't run."

"Maybe. Unless they're framed." Josie shot her a smile. But as she turned to leave, a shadow presented itself on the hallway floor. Someone was listening around the corner. Who? She lowered her voice. "Layla, if I'm right and Dane wasn't the one to murder your husband, surely you realize that could put you in danger. If you ever need to talk…"

The woman glared at her, and Josie could feel Layla's eyes on her as she walked down the pathway. She resisted the urge to turn around until she got to her Bronco. Layla stood on her porch.

When Josie opened her door, she quickly warned under her breath, "Don't get up yet. She's watching."

Dane whispered, "Okay."

As she pulled away, she gave Layla a quick wave before disappearing up the drive and out of the gate. "You can get up now."

He was slow to look out the window back at the house. "How did it go? Did you learn anything?"

"I'm certain someone else was in the house."

Dane sat up straight. "Who?"

She shook her head. "I don't know. I heard a door shut and there was a shadow around the corner."

His gaze took her in. "I didn't see any vehicles, but I probably wouldn't since she has a three-car garage. Did she say who else might be involved?"

"No. She blamed Harlan's death on you. How did you get along with Layla before he died?"

He shrugged. "She was friendly. We got together several times a year, like at the Christmas employee party and then a few times for burgers or barbeque. Mainly, though, I saw Layla when she went to worship services."

"How was that? I mean, did she seem sincere?" Josie couldn't shake the feeling that Layla was a fake. But maybe not. Everyone handled grief differently.

Dane looked thoughtful for a moment. "I have no idea. I've never thought about it, but she was nice enough. She never seemed to mind that Harlan would invite me over or that he included me with their family."

Like a fifth wheel. Josie could fill in the blanks and realized how much Dane had felt like an outcast. At times, she had felt the same way. But it was more than that. She detected the strain in his voice. A glance to him showed him staring out his window. She'd never considered how much he might be grieving for his partner. "You miss him, don't you?"

"Yeah, I do." He nodded. "We used to work together at Red River Construction, and he was my supervisor. After high school, I'd worked several odd jobs and then applied at Red River from an online advertisement. Harlan hired me. Back then, I walked around with a chip on my shoulder and got into arguments with other employees. Harlan called me into his office and had a talk with me. I was expecting to be reprimanded, but he talked to me about needing me to be a part of his team. He complimented me on driving a forklift and that it was beneficial I wasn't afraid of heights."

Josie caught the smile on Dane's lips.

"I was always a kind of daredevil as a kid, and this was the first time someone had said to me it gave me an advantage."

"Yeah, I guess you're right." Something in his demeanor told her Harlan had been much more than a boss.

"He made me feel like I could be a part of a team." Almost as if he read her thoughts, he added, "Harlan invited me to worship services. He never preached to me, but rather, included me. It didn't take long for me to see how much I'd been missing. Gave me purpose besides being angry all the time."

As Josie listened to him, she realized Layla was wrong. Harlan hadn't pitied Dane but had been a sort of mentor to him. There's no way Dane had misinterpreted their relationship. "What made you two go into business together?"

"I'd taken a couple of business classes online and began to want to go out on my own. I know, it was kind of a silly dream."

She looked at him. "Not at all."

He shot her a smile. "I didn't have the money. At first when I mentioned it, Harlan didn't seem interested, but then a local construction company went out of business and was put up for sale. The owner had been young and made poor decisions. Being that Harlan was twenty years older than me, he had no desire to start a business by himself but loved the idea of starting one together. He told me retirement would come soon enough, but he liked the idea of running a company. In his words, he had the capital and connections, I had the energy."

Josie said, "He sounds like a good man."

"You would've liked him. I'm sure of it." He pointed toward his rearview mirror. "That silver GMC has been following you for a while."

"I noticed that, too. It's possible the driver is simply headed to Liberty like us. Our guy back at the cabin drove a black Dodge."

Dane continued to watch.

She switched on her signal and turned off onto a county highway, headed north.

"Where are you going?"

"Just seeing if he is following." She looked in her rearview mirror and the truck whizzed past, continuing on the main road.

He straightened. "I guess you were right. Where to now?"

"Bliss said I could use their place while she's gone. I want to do some digging into Layla's background."

"Really? Something bothering you?"

"Not so much. But I always like to dig into people to see whether they're on the up-and-up or not." When they came to an intersection, she turned right on a road that would take them the back way into Liberty.

"Who do you think was in the house?"

"I don't know. I keep thinking about that. Do you think Layla may have already met someone?"

He shrugged. "It's possible. Harlan seemed happy, but he also wasn't the kind to talk about his personal life."

"So, if Pierce was investigating something, what do you think it was?"

"Again, I don't know. It wouldn't have been the missing thirty thousand dollars because Pierce was hired before the money went missing."

"Yeah, you're right. Maybe it had nothing to do with the money, but something more personal."

Suddenly something appeared in the road, and she didn't have time to swerve. With a loud bang, her passenger-side tire blew, and the SUV pulled to the right. She hit the brakes and fought to keep it on the road.

Dane pulled his gun out. "Do you see anyone?"

She glanced around. Only pastures and trees. "Not yet. Wait—" she pointed "—over there."

A man jumped up from the grass only ten yards away and aimed his gun. At the same time, Dane raised his.

Flat tire or not, she floored the gas.

The Bronco jumped, causing Dane's aim to be off. His shot went high as bullets kicked up dirt behind the SUV. Josie kept the accelerator down even as the wheel went *thwack, thwack,*

thwack, thwack on the pavement. "I don't know where the guy's vehicle is, but I think we're out of reach of his gun."

The back window shattered, causing him to cringe. Josie let out a squeal.

"Are you hit?"

She shook her head. "No, but ever since I took that bullet last year, I have no desire to have a repeat."

He kept watch behind them to see if they were being pursued, but there was no sign of a vehicle.

Dane didn't like the sound of that. He knew a relationship with Josie was unlikely—there would never be trust if she didn't believe his word—but still his stomach tightened at the thought of her being injured—or worse. Maybe it was because she had been his first love, or that he felt partially to blame, but either way, he couldn't let anything happen to her. "I shouldn't have asked."

She laughed. "It's not your fault."

"I know." Again, he checked his mirror, but no one appeared to be following them. A driveway to a ranch house appeared in front of them, and he pointed. "How's your spare?"

"It's a new tire, and it's full size. Not the donut kind."

"Pull in there, and I'll change it for you."

"I can change it myself, but since you offered…" She turned into the drive and moved several yards from the entrance.

She was smart getting off the road. The three doors on the garage were closed and there were no vehicles in the drive. "Doesn't look like there's anyone around, but I'll hurry."

Most people were still friendly in the country and wouldn't mind them being parked there for a few minutes, but one never knew. He got out and noticed the wheel was bent. He hurried to the back and removed the spare from the back door along with the jack and four-way lug nut wrench.

Josie got out and came around to his side of the vehicle. "I hope that didn't damage more than the wheel."

"Doesn't look like it." After he pulled off the wheel, he looked at the tire. "There are spikes in the tread. This was definitely a trap."

She rubbed her wrist across her forehead to wipe off the sweat and looked to the south, the direction they'd just come. "But there was no way for anyone to know we were going to take that road, especially the silver GMC. The driver must have called his partner."

"That makes sense." He hurriedly put on the new tire and had started to tighten down the lug nuts when a vehicle showed in the distance.

"Dane. Looks like we have company."

"I see them." He spun the tool fast and tightened it as much as he could. As he slid on the last nut, the approaching vehicle's engine roared.

"Come on. We've got to go. You can finish that later." Josie slammed the driver's side door shut.

Dane threw the ruined tire and the tool into the back seat as he jumped in.

"I'll have to turn around in a minute." She took off down the driveway toward the rancher's house. The front door opened, and a lady came out with a baby on her hip, a look of curiosity on her face.

"Oh, no."

"Turn around. Turn around." Dane hung on as Josie whipped into the adjoining pasture. "I didn't mean to go into the pasture."

"I'm trying to get far away from the house."

The silver GMC barreled down the driveway and then whipped into the same open gate Josie had used.

"Here he comes. You need to get back on the road."

She gritted her teeth. "I'm trying. I didn't want to meet them head-on in the lady's driveway."

"I wasn't criticizing." He held on as she flew across the rough terrain. The Bronco approached a narrow but deep washout. "Watch out."

The front tires hit hard and then half bounced, half flew across the opening and landed with a jolt. Glancing his way, she said, "I've driven my fair share of backroads in my time. You're not the only one who can jump a ditch."

"It's scarier in the passenger seat. I'd rather

you not show me what it feels like to drive on two wheels, though."

A grove of trees appeared in front of them.

Her teeth gritted as she sped between two trees. When they came out on the other side, the pickup was farther back. She floored it again and raced along a barbwire fence. She plowed through it and got back on the road. "I'll find out who the owner is and pay him later."

"I don't care as long as we leave these guys behind."

"My thoughts exactly."

After they had gone another mile, she turned to him. "Why do you think these guys just keep coming after us? I mean, I know they want us dead, but so far, the attacks have been away from others."

"I noticed that, too. Could be that when they find us, we just happen to be in remote areas."

She nodded. "Yeah. Or others would recognize him, and he doesn't want to take the chance of being recognized."

"Could be, but I don't want to bet my life on it."

"Me either."

Dane continued to keep a look out for the silver truck, but there were no more sightings.

As they came to the edge of town, Josie said, "I'm going to drop by the tire shop to get a new one."

Dane waited in the Bronco while the technician retrieved the wheel out of the back, and he said he'd be an hour before he had a new tire mounted.

Josie turned to him. "Would you like to get something to eat while we wait?"

"I'm starving, so yeah."

"Okay. There's a burger place over there within walking distance. I'll pick up something for Hattie and Everly. Hattie must work the afternoon shift, so I'll need to do something."

He climbed out of the SUV and walked over to her.

"I don't mind having a deputy watch Everly, but I would rather have someone closer to me keep an eye on her until this case is wrapped up."

"You mean like your grandpa?"

"Yeah."

As they walked beside each other, Dane kept a watch out for the silver truck. There was no way around this. Leaving the girl at a retirement home would not be his first option. But they had little choice with danger hitting them at every turn. Until this man was caught, none of them would be safe again.

FOURTEEN

The glass door opened as Phillip, the doorman, stepped aside. "Good afternoon, Miss Hunt."

"Hello, Phillip." She shot him a smile. It made her feel better to know security was at least present at the retirement home.

The door closed silently behind her. The padded carpet felt good under her feet, and the cool air was fresh and welcoming. But when the lady at the reception desk did a double take as she walked past with Everly, Josie figured she should've cleaned up before she came by. There simply wasn't time. She plastered on a smile. "Good afternoon."

"Afternoon." The woman's smile feigned cheer. "Your grandfather is in the rec room."

Josie glanced down at her dirty wrist. Had she gotten grime on her face? Her hair hung in her face, and it tended to curl when damp. A glance down to her work boots made her almost laugh. When she was younger, she remembered her grandfather's mannerisms would embarrass her sometimes. Now, here she was in his retirement home doing the same thing.

A group of men was sitting at a table playing dominoes when she entered. A tall, white-haired man in the middle glanced up. As she approached, his eyes lit up.

"Josie Sue." He looked from her boots to the top of her head. "Been out mudding?"

"Ha, ha, Grandpa. Not really."

He nodded a greeting toward Everly. "Hello, young lady."

"Hi." Everly glanced shyly at the group.

"Can I talk with you?" As the rest of the guys looked on, Josie added, "Alone."

Bill, a man in his nineties, scrutinized her. Some of her grandpa's friends had been in law enforcement or worked in law offices. She didn't know who worked where, but they all enjoyed telling stories about the good old days and tended to complain about recent times. Judges. Lawyers. The laws. The DA. Schools. Politics. Nothing was off limits in the complaint department.

Her grandpa climbed to his feet. "Certainly. Come here and give your grandpa a hug."

Josie stepped his way, and he wrapped his arm around her and squeezed. The smell of his shirt brought back good memories. The action made her want to cry and tell him all of her problems just like she had when she was a girl, but she held back.

"Come on back to my room."

She walked beside him, holding Everly's hand. Even though her grandpa still kept up a decent pace, he'd slowed a bit since the last time she'd visited him. He opened the door to his room, and they filed in. She turned to Everly, leaning over and placing her hands on her shoulders.

"Wait here by the door. I'll be right back."

Everly nodded, her eyes wide, and Josie knew she had to make this quick.

She went in her grandfather's living room, to where she could still see Everly.

He turned to her. "What's going on?"

"I need help," she whispered.

"Does this have to do with that sweet girl you adopted?"

He struggled to remember Everly's name. "It does. I just learned her daddy, Pierce Browning, was murdered and Everly witnessed it."

"Are you sure?" His eyebrows knitted in concern as he glanced back at her.

She nodded. "Positive. I took her to the police station, and she went through mug shots. There were several men she identified as looking like the man, but none were conclusive."

He gave a slow whistle and shook his head. "What is wrong with people? Why would someone do that? I will never understand what causes someone to hurt or kill another. You'd think I was used to it by now, but a person should never grow accustomed to evil."

Her grandpa could complain about this for several minutes, so she interrupted. "I need help."

His face softened. "Are you in danger?"

"No. Yes. I need you to watch Everly for me. Whoever killed Pierce realizes she can identify him. I don't know who the killer is, but we believe he also killed Dane's business partner."

He frowned, making his wrinkles bunch up. "Dane Haggerty? Please tell me you're not talking to that boy again."

"Grandpa, he's twenty-eight years old. He's hardly a boy." She didn't want to talk about Dane, but it was only fair if he was going to keep an eye on Everly that he understood what was at stake. "I don't know if you heard, but Dane was accused of—"

"Killed his partner." He cut her off while his face turned red. "There's a warrant for his arrest. He's not the kind of man I want you hanging around. Especially with my great-granddaughter."

She planted her hand on her hip and cocked her head to the side. "Would you please trust that you raised a smart lady?"

"I know that," he said irritably.

"I don't have much time. But I need you to keep her inside."

"Where is Sheriff Van Carroll? Surely, he can give you protection."

"He's out of town. Kennedy and Silas from my team are here."

"I want you to stay with me. Let the authorities do their job."

She smiled. "I would love to, but I can't sit back and wait. I'm the best person to find this guy. The sooner he's off of the streets, the safer me and Everly will be."

"I still say you're better off with me. And it's more than that. Several of the old gang are here."

"I know." She patted him on the chest. "I love you, Grandpa. Please keep an eye on her."

"I love you, too."

She looked over her shoulder and waved at Everly to enter. "Come on."

Everly gave a hesitant smile as she hurried over to him.

A door shut from somewhere close, and then Dane glanced around the corner before stepping into the room. "We appreciate this. Please know that I'll do everything I can to keep your granddaughter safe."

Totally ignoring him, Grandpa looked back at her. "Are you sure this is how you want it?"

"Yes. He's innocent."

The older man shook his head, before looking back at Dane. He pointed. "Don't let her get hurt. I'm warning you."

Her chest tightened. Her grandfather had been a strong man when younger, but he didn't realize he was getting older.

Thankfully, Dane had the sense to nod. "Yes, sir."

Doubts whether she should leave Everly there plagued her. But she'd gone over this in her mind multiple times. There was no easy solution. The retirement home allowed residents to have overnight guests. She leaned down and got close. "Your great grandpa is going to take good care of you. If you need anything, ask him. Do you understand?"

"I'll be fine."

"Okay. Listen to him. You have my phone number?"

"I do. It's in my pocket." She gave Josie a little push. "Go."

As she caught up to Dane and they walked toward the back exit, she turned back for one more look and gave her a little wave.

Please, Lord, watch over Everly and Grandpa.

They walked out and got in the Bronco. After she shut the door and started the engine, warmth touched her hand. She glanced down at Dane's hand on hers.

"Everly will be fine."

She looked into his serious brown eyes. "I realize you're trying to help, but you can't know that."

"But I prayed to God. No matter what happens, everything will turn out for the best."

She let out a loud sigh and pulled her hand back then put it on the steering wheel. "I've always believed in God, as did my parents, and Grandpa. But I'm scared. It may be wrong, but I can't help but worry about her safety."

"You wouldn't be human if you didn't. Let's go find this guy."

Dane's words did help a little. The quicker the killer was arrested, the sooner she could get on with her life. As she traveled across town to the edge of Liberty, she passed a parking lot and noticed a silver GMC traveling fast toward the exit. A white coupe braked in front of her, causing her almost to rear-end the car. "Did you see that?"

"Silver truck? Yeah." Dane turned sideways in his seat as he looked through the back window. "He's headed the other direction."

"Oh no, you don't." She whipped into the next available parking lot and turned around. When there was a break in the traffic, she gassed it and headed in the same direction as the truck. "Do you see him?"

"Not yet." Dane leaned forward. "He didn't turn down that street. Wait. There. He disappeared behind that building." He pointed at a large empty building that used to be a grocery store.

Josie followed his directions and sped across

the bare pavement. This wasn't the best part of town, but she didn't want to lose this guy. "Do you think he was following us? Like he saw where I dropped Everly off?"

"I don't know. That question crossed my mind, too."

As she approached the corner of the building, she slowed and eased into the back alley. There was no sign of the vehicle. "Where did he go?"

Dane twisted, looking around. "I don't see him. Ease forward. We know he went to the left."

She did as he said, her heart racing in her chest. Something wasn't right. Had the guy seen her? She reached down to her ankle holster to retrieve her gun as her driver's side window exploded.

"Get down!"

She ducked and then yanked on the wheel, slamming the Bronco into a trash dumpster. She fumbled to put the vehicle into Reverse as tires squealed on pavement.

"Stay down." Dane peeked over the seat and fired two shots through the broken window.

It was a trap, and she'd fallen right into it.

Fierce protectiveness came over Dane as he searched for the gunman. The man had fired from somewhere between the narrow space among two buildings but had disappeared. If Josie hadn't leaned down, she probably would've taken at least one bullet.

His blood pumped through his veins at an alarming rate. "Let me drive." At the scowl he received, he added, "I know it's your vehicle, but you're a better shooter than me, and I'm capable of driving. There's no time for discussion."

Her face paled, but she nodded and quickly climbed over the console as he scooted to the driver's seat. He didn't move as smoothly with his long legs, but it was better than being in the open.

He put the Bronco in gear and eased forward, until he was even with the narrow alley between the structures. It was empty except for trash littering the ground. Continuing forward, he looked for the silver pickup. It had to be close. The next building had a shop door. He stopped. "I'm going to check this out. If we were lured here, I want to know who's setting the bait."

She nodded. "I'll cover you."

They got out at the same time, and he waited for her to get into position at the front of her SUV. He nodded before reaching down and yanking the shop door handle up. The door squeaked as it rolled open.

The GMC sat inside with the bed facing him. There was no one inside that he could see. He mouthed, "I'm going to check it out" once more.

She moved closer with her gun ready.

The bay was narrow, not leaving much of a path. After peering under the vehicle to make certain no feet could be seen underneath the carriage, he approached the driver's side door while keeping his eyes on the front seat. With his gun aimed, he glanced inside. Empty.

He looked back at Josie and shook his head, telling her no one was inside. Suddenly, a jacked-up Ford Raptor pulled up in the alley behind them. Josie turned her back to Dane and her arm fell to her side, with her palm facing him as she waved him backward.

Was she trying to tell him to stay back? Dane hunched down and moved toward the front of the pickup.

A stocky man wearing a baseball cap, jeans and running shoes stepped out of the vehicle. Muscles bulged from beneath his T-shirt. He slammed the door and strutted over to her. "Josie, you are a hard person to track down."

Even though the man was slightly turned, and his facial details not clear, Dane knew his identity.

"How can I help you, Tyler?" Josie cocked her head to the side—a telling move when she was annoyed.

Big Tyler Jorgenson. Dane had only viewed pictures and heard stories of the rough, not-by-the-book bounty hunter.

"I need help finding someone who has a warrant for his arrest. Dane Haggerty. Have you seen him?"

"What makes you think I've seen him?" Josie stalled.

Dane slowly stepped back deeper into the shop until he made it to the front of the vehicle. With Harlan's killer targeting them, the last thing he needed to worry about was a bounty hunter trying to bring him in. A door stood on the other side of the shelves, and Dane moved closer.

"The sheriff's department over in McCade County had a report of an exchange of gunfire. Your name was mentioned along with Haggerty's."

"I wish I could help you."

The large bounty hunter frowned at her. "You wouldn't be protecting him, would you, Hunt? I heard your daughter was in danger. I would think the safest thing for everyone would be if I brought him in. After I receive my payment, he can trust his fate to the law."

Anger tugged at Dane as he restrained himself from pummeling Tyler for bringing Everly into this fight—not that he would fare well in a physical confrontation with the brawny man. He didn't want Josie to be tempted to lie for him. Gently, he turned the knob and eased the door open, sunlight pouring in. He stepped out of the room and to the front of the building. The parking lot was empty. He had no idea where the driver of the silver GMC had gone, but his gut told him he was still nearby.

Unless he'd taken another vehicle after stashing the truck. But there hadn't been enough time.

Or maybe he and Josie had been so intent on seeing where the truck had gone, they'd missed a man on foot.

He wasn't certain of anything except that they needed to be ready for the unexpected.

Dane hurried along the storefronts while keeping aware of the parking lot and the buildings as he passed by each one. At the last store— an empty tile and floor-covering business—he stopped and peeked around the corner.

Nothing.

In front of him lay a few trees and a narrow rock road leading to a building. He glanced around the corner again to make sure it was clear and then dashed toward three scraggly trees. Instead of stopping to look back, he wove through the brush and came out near the driveway. The metal building was an old car wash with two bays. The hoses were gone, and graffiti covered the walls.

He skirted to the far side of the trees and hurried across the driveway to the protection of the car wash. From that vantage point, he could see the backside of the building he'd just vacated. Josie remained beside her vehicle. The bounty hunter was gone, but his truck was still there.

Josie appeared relaxed but then she looked over her shoulder toward him. Had she seen where he'd gone?

A few seconds later, a tall man came out of the

front of the last building and proceeded around the corner. When he got to the back edge of the building, he peered about. He wore dark clothes and held something in his hand. Josie had her back turned toward the man.

"Look behind you, Josie," Dane whispered under his breath.

The suspect raised his gun, and Dane did the same. He'd never shot anyone before, but he would not sit there and watch a killer shoot Josie.

The man stepped out from around the corner just as the bounty hunter came from the far side of the building.

"Look out, Josie!"

Her head snapped up, and Dane pulled the trigger. A bullet hit above the suspect's head and into the brick building. The guy rolled for cover on the ground.

Josie dashed for the passenger side of her vehicle.

Tyler Jorgenson's attention went to the gunman and then to Dane's direction.

Dane ran through the wash bay and into the steep gully on the other side. He half slid and half fell to the bottom, his boots landing with a splash. The stream was only about a foot deep, but he took off through the ditch as fast as he could move.

Tires squealed.

That was probably Big Tyler coming for him,

but he wished it were Josie. His thoughts went to her as he trucked through marshy ground. He hoped the gunman didn't come after her, and after being shot at, the man would be more likely cautious with his moves. Josie knew her stuff, and he had to trust her to get away from this guy.

Up ahead was a large metal culvert, about three feet in diameter. He started to go in and hide, but if Tyler crossed this way, it would be the first place he searched. Dane crawled back up the bank on the far side to take a look.

Tyler's Ford Raptor raced down the road. The land was grassy here. Taking a chance, he climbed out of the gully and ran as fast as he could while staying low. The highway crossed in front of him, and a bridge lay to his right.

He sprinted for it.

He glanced over his left shoulder to see Tyler stop and check the tinhorn. No doubt the truck would catch him quickly, but not if he weren't spotted. His breath came in pants, but adrenaline kept him going. As his side began to ache, he stood straight to ease the discomfort.

Tyler's truck was headed his way, the engine revving as rocks spewed.

Sirens sounded in the distance.

Dane didn't turn to look but ran. The rumble of the approaching vehicle and the sirens grew louder. Only a few more yards to the bridge. With all his might, he ran to the middle of the bridge. The river flowed at a lazy rate beneath him.

"Dane Haggerty, I'm taking you in for the murder of Harlan Schmidt. Stop. Put your hands above your head."

The bounty hunter's command rang through his mind, but Dane had no intention of being arrested today. He prayed the man would not shoot him, and his instincts told him he had to get away if he wanted to survive.

FIFTEEN

Josie's chest tightened as she watched the bounty hunter take off after Dane. With her gun still in her hand, she ran around her Bronco and climbed into the driver's seat. She fired it up and took off. As she approached the corner of the building, movement caught her eye from the left. She jerked the wheel just as a bullet whizzed past her head and into the dash.

She fired out of her window at the man huddled on the sidewalk. She didn't know if she hit him, but a glance in her rearview mirror said he didn't follow her. She wanted to help Dane, but the gunman needed to be brought down. If Dane was arrested, she'd have to do everything in her power to find the true killer so he would be exonerated. Working with law enforcement had taught her that.

She turned her Bronco around and readied her gun as she approached the building. The man wasn't in sight, but he had to be close. She looked around, not wanting him to sneak up on her.

Using the speaker on her phone, she called 9-1-1. Deputies were already close, but they needed to know Pierce's killer suspect was there. All she had to do was subdue him until they arrived. When the dispatcher answered, Josie quickly relayed her location and the information about the shooter. She didn't stay on the line.

After she disconnected, she drove around to the back of the building where she'd been only minutes before. The man must be going back for his truck. She stopped and slid out of the Bronco. Making her way to the back, she skirted around the bumper and to the passenger side. Poised to shoot, she approached the garage opening.

She peeked around the edge.

Sure enough, a man sat behind the wheel and started the truck. Tinted windows kept her from identifying the man, but he appeared tall like the man in the woods the first night.

In her peripheral vision she saw a deputy's truck was headed this way.

She wasn't an officer, but she couldn't let the man simply drive away. Nor could she just shoot him. In a flash, she hurried back to her Bronco and pulled forward, blocking the man's escape.

Her prized Bronco had been her dad's many years ago, and she hated the thought of wrecking it. She would do what she had to.

The man threw his truck into gear. Instead of ramming her vehicle, he shot backward, slammed into the shelves knocking them over before crashing through the back wall.

"No. No. No." Her foot hit the accelerator, and her SUV jumped forward. She tore around the building, down the alley, and to the front. The man's silver GMC flew onto the highway, and other motorists' tires squealed as they hit their brakes and one car went into the ditch to avoid a crash.

By the time Josie got to the highway, he passed three cars on the shoulder before returning to the road. When a break in the traffic appeared, she pulled out. But the man was so determined to get away, he passed a car while a semitruck was headed his way in oncoming traffic. The big rig driver jerked the wheel to the shoulder and halfway in the grass to avoid hitting him.

"He's going to kill an innocent person." At the next driveway, she pulled in and turned around, heading back to the building. A deputy's pickup crossed the pavement and stopped by her Bronco. The man exited his vehicle and strode over.

She rolled down her window. "The suspect got away. He traveled that way in a newer model silver GMC truck driving erratic. I decided to let the authorities find him."

"Are you Miss Hunt?" At her nod, he continued. "That was smart thinking. We'll find him. Stick around. I'm certain one of the other deputies will need to talk with you."

When he got back into his vehicle, she saw him talking on his handheld radio. He turned on his lights and took off in pursuit.

As she headed in the direction Dane had gone, she couldn't help but believe the deputy wouldn't be able to catch the suspect. There had been no need to stop and speak to her since she'd relayed the information to the dispatcher. Frustration tugged at her. Was this guy ever going to be caught?

She sped down the narrow road past the car wash until she came out on the highway. Tyler's big truck, along with two deputies' vehicles, sat on a bridge about a half mile away. Two men appeared to be looking over the edge.

Oh no. What happened? Please tell her Dane didn't jump.

Blood thumped through her ears as she prepared for the worst. She parked behind a deputy's truck and hurried to the edge of the bridge.

She asked the deputies, "What happened?"

"Looks like our man jumped off the bridge."

Josie managed to keep her intake of breath quiet. Her gaze sought out movement in the shallow creek. The bridge was at least thirty feet high, but the water wasn't that deep.

One of the male deputies she didn't recognize stared at her. "I have to wonder, Miss Hunt. Did you know Dane was with you all along?"

Ignoring him, she looked at the female deputy. "Deputy Perkins, do you know what happened?"

"Maybe I should ask you the same thing." Hattie's tone carried reproach.

Not wanting to say anything that could be used against her, Josie shrugged.

Tyler climbed up the side of the riverbank. "No sign of him. I'll find him."

Josie stood back and let the man pass on his way to his truck. He slammed the door and took off, his tires squealing. On the other side of the river, the Raptor turned and raced along a dirt trail by the bank. She held her breath as a huge cloud of dust filled the air and then dissipated.

The male deputy talked on his cell phone a few feet away and then hurried to his truck. Before he climbed in, he said to Deputy Perkins, "I'm taking the highway and am going further downstream."

"Okay." After he pulled away, Perkins turned to her. "If you're hiding Haggerty, you know you can be arrested for harboring a fugitive."

"Yes, ma'am." The deputy's words hung in the air as Josie climbed into her Bronco. The day kept getting worse. First, she'd lost Pierce's killer, and now Dane tried to escape. There was no way to make that jump in the shallow without getting hurt. With Tyler on one side of the river and the deputy on the other, he'd be lucky if he wasn't arrested in the next few minutes.

As much as she didn't want to involve herself in his case, she whipped the Bronco onto the path Tyler had taken to turn around. When she started to back up, she glanced in the rearview mirror, and a face was staring back at her.

She squealed and put her hand to her chest. "Dane Haggerty. You scared me half to death."

"Get me out of here."

"You've got some explaining to do." She glanced around to make certain no deputies were still in the area. "I'd like to know how you got into my vehicle when you were nowhere to be found when I pulled up."

Dane remained hunched down in case someone was still nearby. "I thought I was caught. I started to jump into the river, but decided I'd probably break my neck because it was too shallow."

"You think?"

"I jumped to the bank and crawled to the other side under the bridge. Then I hid in the bed of Perkins's pickup."

Josie's jaw dropped. "You've got to be kidding me. That was taking a big chance."

"Not so much. She was the last vehicle here until you arrived. Chances were no one would be walking by the bed of her truck. Then you pulled up. While you were watching Tyler, I climbed in here."

She shook her head. "You haven't changed much since high school. You've always taken risks."

"Not really," he answered quickly. He didn't like her believing he was still the same immature teen he was in school. "I prefer to believe I've done well in business, especially with Harlan's help. But the old survival instincts kick in when I feel the walls closing in."

Again, she stared at him in the mirror. For two long seconds, they stared at one another until she looked back to the road. "Where to?"

"I'd like to look for that silver GMC, but since the deputy is in pursuit, we probably need to let them do their job. Did you get a good look at the guy?"

"A side view, but I didn't recognize him or get a good enough look to give a description."

"Yeah. It's like he knows if we see him, we'll recognize him. That could be a good lead."

She nodded and came to a stop at a red light at a main intersection on the edge of town. "It only makes sense since he knew Pierce and Harlan. Do you think it's someone we both know?"

The way she said it insinuated more. "You mean like someone we went to school with?"

She shrugged. "Could be. Since we haven't worked together since we graduated, that would be the most common denominator."

The DA's son kept returning to his mind. But

why target Harlan and Pierce? He leaned forward. "I want to check out the DA's son." At her funny look, he replied, "What?"

"Nothing."

"No. Say what you're thinking."

She sighed. "You better have a great reason for mentioning him to others or it's going to look like revenge for the car incident."

"Josie, that was years ago. Yes, I was mad back then, real mad, for being accused and charged with theft. Keaton Stebbins set me up on purpose. When I tried to tell the judge that, he didn't listen. Nobody did. But I've moved on now. The only thing that bothers me is when people still assume I'm guilty of crimes without proof. It tends to get old."

The light turned green, and she took off. "What makes you think he's involved?"

"I don't, necessarily. First, not many people know I was charged with theft because I was a minor. The record was sealed. Someone stays one step ahead of me."

"Like they have inside knowledge? Come on. That seems like a stretch. Pierce was investigating something for Harlan, and he's in construction. What does that have to do with law enforcement?"

"I don't know yet. Stebbins is on the city building committee." Even as Dane said the words, he wasn't certain of a connection. What could it be?

Kickbacks? "You're an investigator. Can you find out what he was working on?"

"I will. But I'll need to be discreet. A person can get a bad rep for stepping on the toes of those in the upper crust, especially those in law enforcement."

"I hear you." Dane smiled.

"Do you? I mean, really hear me." Her gaze cut to him. "I could get into trouble, Dane. I have a daughter to think about. You plan to adopt Violet. Everything you do needs to be on the up-and-up."

He knew this was coming. She wanted him to turn himself in. What if it backfired? What if he spent the rest of his life in prison for a crime he didn't commit?

Josie's eyebrows rose in question. "Do you trust me?"

Dane stared at her. "That has nothing to do—"

"I was once told it was simple question." She looked at him with a quirked eyebrow, and repeated, "Do you trust me?"

He nodded. "Yeah, I trust you."

A smile crept across Josie's face. "Good. Then please agree to see Sheriff Van Carroll. I'll go with you."

"He's out of town."

She shook her head. "He got back this morning."

Dane sighed. "I'll do it."

"Good. I've already called him and he's expecting you to contact him."

Dane clenched his teeth realizing that she knew he'd agree. His mind warred with itself. Part of him would be glad to quit running and hopefully have help. The other part was scared to death he'd regret his decision. He always remembered Harlan would tell him to have faith. Maybe this was what it felt like. A little scary, but hope danced in front of him.

Josie's cell phone rang as she pulled into Bliss's drive and parked beside Dane's motorcycle. She glanced at the screen. "It's Layla."

Dane's gaze connected with hers before he moved close so he could hear.

She hit Accept and put it on speaker while holding the phone between them. He didn't back away even though there was no need to be this close. The warmth of his breath felt good.

"Hello. This is Josie."

"I need to talk to you." Layla's voice sounded strained. "I have evidence."

The prospect of having good news had her holding her breath to see if Layla's news would finally wrap this case up.

Josie asked, "What did you find?"

"I'd rather not talk to you over the phone. I need to see you in person."

She and Dane exchanged looks. "Are you certain? If I knew what you—"

"I can't talk on the phone. Come right now to my house."

"Okay. I'll see you in a bit." She disconnected and then faced Dane. "What do you think this is about?"

"I don't know, but we need answers now. I'm going with you."

She shook her head. "Go turn yourself in. Violet is depending on you. When the killer is caught, I want you to be free. The longer you run, the harder it will be to clear your name."

His jaw tensed. "I don't like this. It could be a trap. It's too risky."

"I'm armed and trained. I'll call you as soon as I learn something."

"Not good enough, Josie. I can turn myself in after you meet with Layla, I promise."

She shook her head. "No. You have a bounty hunter on your tail who doesn't care if he takes you alive. You'll be safer under the sheriff's protection."

She whispered, "Trust me."

For several seconds their eyes connected. Dane leaned down and his lips touched hers in a light kiss.

After he pulled back, she could still feel his touch on her. "Be careful."

He shoved his baseball cap on his head. "I will. I'm ready to get there."

She followed him out the door and watched

as he got on his bike and rode to the end of the driveway. He turned and gave her one more look before pulling out onto the road.

Please, Lord, be with Dane. Help him to learn to trust.

SIXTEEN

Dane dreaded talking with Sheriff Van Carroll. Even though Josie assured him he was not going to remain in jail, he couldn't help but think this might be a mistake. Would the sheriff lie to Josie? Maybe.

Josie kept talking about trust. Could he ever have faith in anyone again? He wanted to believe her. And to gain her trust, he was willing to take a chance on the authorities.

The wind blowing on his face felt cool and unfettered. He prayed this was not the last time he was free. He couldn't fail this time.

A car in front of him slowed, and he eased around it. The lady inside was talking on her cell phone. After he pulled back into his lane, the highway opened to not much traffic. As he tried to prepare his mind for his talk with the sheriff, he went over the details of the case and anticipated possible questions.

A shadow stretched from behind him. He checked his mirror and saw the grille of a pickup grow large before it rammed into him. His back tire swerved before he got it back under control. He gassed it, but something was wrong with his bike. The machine shook and veered to the left. The impact must've bent his wheel. He could've recovered, but then he was hit again.

He held on, but the back tire swung around to his left and slid on the pavement. The front tire dug in and then he flew forward, slapping his face against his mirrors before landing hard on the shoulder of the highway. Painful shock waves reverberated through his body. His shoulder hit first, followed by his helmet slamming the ground. His right eye stung, forcing him to squint against the agony. He ripped off his helmet.

The squeal of brakes added to the ringing in his head.

He scrambled to his feet, fell, and then got back up. He only took a couple of steps before someone seized him from behind. He grabbed for his gun in the back of his waistband, but before he reached it, strong hands manhandled him by the shirt and hauled him to the silver truck. Then he was shoved into the passenger seat.

Dane swung his fist at the man. It was a glancing blow. He tried to get his breath and swallow down the pain that continued to pulse through his body. He punched at him again, but his fist was knocked aside.

"You've been asking for this." Something hard

jabbed him in the side. "You make a fast move, and I'll blow you away. Just so you don't try anything stupid, Josie and the girl are depending on you."

The gruff, familiar voice had him straining to look into the angry blue eyes of his captor. Alec Hickman. No doubt he'd love to pull the trigger of the pistol sticking him in the gut. The man hurried around to the driver's side of the truck.

A glance to the back seat showed no one. Thankful Josie or Everly weren't taken by Alec gave Dane time to clear his head and think. What did he mean Josie and Everly were depending on him?

Had Alec captured them? If so, where was he holding them?

Dane still had his gun, but he needed to use it at the right time now that he knew the killer's identity.

A couple of cars stopped on the highway to check out the wreck, but Alec spun his truck around, almost hitting a teen dressed in a baseball uniform. The kid held his cell phone up, evidently snapping photos of them. Even if authorities were notified, there was a good chance it'd be too late to help Dane.

"Why did you kill Harlan?"

Hickman scowled as he looked at him. "The cold-hearted man shouldn't have fired me. He could've given me a second chance. Because of you two, my wife left me."

Alec blamed Dane also? Both he and Harlan had been doing their jobs. Alec had a drinking problem that made him a liability to keep with the company. This meant Alec had no intention of letting him live. He needed to get a message to Josie or the sheriff's department. He dropped his right hand to the seat beside him and slowly eased it toward his gun. His fingers touched the butt, but he couldn't withdraw it without being noticeable. He leaned forward to block the view from Hickman. To keep his attention diverted, Dane spoke while he withdrew the weapon. "You were drinking on the job."

The man slammed on his brakes and pointed at him. "It was one time. I didn't deserve it."

Fury shown in the man's eyes as he took back off on the highway, and Dane knew he'd struck a nerve. Actually, he'd come to work intoxicated numerous times. The last time was the nail in the coffin. Dane's cell phone buzzed in his back pocket.

Alec's head jerked toward him. "Hand over the phone."

In one move, he put his weapon on the seat and raised his left hand in the air as if in surrender while his right removed his phone. He placed it on the dash.

The man's eyes narrowed and then a funny

look crossed his face. He yanked the wheel to the shoulder of the road and stopped. A pistol appeared in his hand. "Give me the gun."

Dane had never been much of a hunter, but there had been a time when he practiced shooting at targets attached to a tree and even gotten skilled at shooting disks. He'd never been good at backing away from a fight either. His hand came up with the Glock and aimed. "No."

Both men pointed their guns at each other while less than two feet away. At this distance, both would die should they fire.

Sweat beaded across Alec's lip, and his eyes grew with rage.

Dane's heart stampeded in his chest. He'd had enough. And Josie still didn't know who the killer was. He couldn't take the chance of Alec getting to her and Everly. The man had big plans to take all of them down; no doubt he hadn't considered he might not come out of this alive. "Well, what's it going to be?"

Right then and there, they both had a decision to make. And Dane prayed with all his might that he'd made the right move because others were depending on him.

Josie was ready to learn something of value. She climbed into her Bronco and took off. Layla's place was about a twenty-minute drive. Time crawled as her mind tried to figure out what evidence Layla had found. Concern for Everly continued to nag at her. Hopefully, her grandpa would keep her safe and they could all go home after Pierce's killer was found and arrested.

Home. It had burned down. Where would they start over? What must it be like for Everly to lose her only remaining parent and then when she does get adopted by an almost stranger, your house is lost in a fire and you must start over again. Kids were resilient, but she knew this was pushing the sentiment too far. Josie had heard the saying many times after her family perished. She prayed nightly Everly would have an easier recovery than what she had experienced.

When she pulled into Layla's drive, the first thing she noticed was her car was parked outside instead of inside the garage like before. No other vehicles were around. She pulled behind Layla's luxury vehicle and walked swiftly to the front door. A quick hit to the doorbell, and she waited.

No answer.

After a few more seconds, she tried again. Still with no response, she tried the door and it opened. "Layla. It's me. I'm coming in."

She stepped inside and called her name again. Even though Layla had asked her to come over, she hated walking into someone's house. The dining area was empty, and she turned toward the living room.

A gasp escaped her. Layla lay on the floor, a

golf-size bump on her head. Blood stained the carpet. "Layla."

Josie felt for a pulse. A faint thump was her return. Immediately, she hit three numbers on her cell phone.

"9-1-1. What's your emergency?"

"I have an unconscious victim with a bump on her head." The dispatcher asked a couple of questions and Josie gave her the address. Against the dispatcher's instructions, Josie informed her she couldn't stay on the line and hung up. Then she called Dane, but it immediately went to voicemail.

A bad feeling came over her. It wasn't like him not to answer, but maybe he was talking with Sheriff Van Carroll and didn't want to interrupt the visit. Josie had worked for the sheriff for years, and after she explained the situation, he agreed if Dane came in, he could have him on bail in a couple of hours, and then Dane could work with authorities instead of running.

She called the sheriff's department.

"Jarvis County sheriff's department."

Josie quickly explained about needing to talk with Dane to the person manning the desk.

"I'm sorry, ma'am, but he hasn't arrived yet."

Her chest tightened. Maybe he had talked with the sheriff and the dispatcher simply didn't know. "May I speak with Sheriff Van Carroll?"

"I'll put you through."

He answered on the first ring. "Van Carroll."

"This is Josie. Have you spoken with Dane Haggerty yet?"

"I'm waiting for him to get here. What's going on? You sound worried."

"He left over thirty minutes ago. He should've already arrived." She told him about Layla's call and finding her on the floor. "The paramedics are on their way."

The sheriff said, "If Haggerty arrives, I'll have him call you."

"Thank you." As soon as she disconnected, she checked on Layla again. Her breathing was still shallow, and her face was pasty white. For fear there might be other injuries, she didn't move the woman's body. While waiting for the paramedics, she decided to look around for a weapon, but none was found in the living room. A person had been here yesterday, so she walked through the house to see if there was anything to tell her the identity of Layla's visitor.

When she stepped into what appeared to be the main bedroom, she noted the bed was made. There were no pictures of Harlan. Maybe the woman wasn't the type to hang photos. She opened the nightstand, and a wallet-sized photo of Layla with a man rested in the bottom of the drawer. Josie had seen pictures of Harlan, but this wasn't him. When Josie checked the bathroom, men's deodorant and an electric shaver were on the counter.

Was Layla already seeing someone? It had only been four months. Some people moved on quickly after losing a spouse, but it made Josie wonder if she had been seeing someone before her husband's death. As she walked back through the home, she passed an office with glass doors. The desk was clear of clutter or stacks of paper, but a soft-sided briefcase sat in the leather chair. It could be Harlan's. Sirens sounded from outside, and she hurried to the front door to meet them.

After two female and one male paramedic came inside, Josie stepped back into the kitchen and texted Dane to call her.

Her phone rang, and she couldn't help but be disappointed to see Silas Boone's name instead of Dane's. "Please tell me you learned something."

"We found a match on the man Everly saw. Alec Hickman, an old employee of Harlan and Dane's. I'm sending you his photo."

A text came through on her cell phone. This was the same man who was pictured with Layla. "Alec was their employee? I didn't know that."

"Do you know him?"

"Not really. I just saw a picture of him at Layla's house." She went on to explain how she found Layla after the woman had called claiming she had some kind of evidence and then about Dane not answering his phone.

"That's not good. Where's your daughter?"

Josie closed her eyes and took a deep breath. She'd been thinking about her, praying for her and Grandpa's safety. "She's staying with my grandpa at the retirement home. I felt that was safer than being with me."

"If you send me the address, I'll send Kennedy to stay with them until we see this case to an end."

Relief fell on her. "I'll do that. Thank you."

"Sure. I found an address for Hickman and I'm on my way to check it out."

"Let me know what you learn." After she disconnected, she sent the retirement home's information to Kennedy and then returned to the living room to find it empty. A look out the front door showed Layla being loaded into the awaiting ambulance. She hurried to her Bronco and was able to leave before the ambulance was ready to go.

Would Hickman be at his home? Possible, but it seemed unlikely to Josie. Even though the sheriff said he'd have Dane call, she tried the department one more time to make certain he hadn't shown up. The dispatcher put her straight through.

"Have you heard from him?"

Josie shook her head as she talked on the phone. "No, and I'm worried."

"Haggerty better not have run again."

"That's not it," she was quick to reply, amazed

at how fast she felt protective over the fugitive. "Texas Ranger Silas Boone just called and said he found a match for the man Everly described. Alec Hickman."

"Hickman. Name sounds familiar."

"He worked with Harlan and Dane several years ago. Silas is on his way to his house as we speak. I'm going to check out the North Texas Custom Builder's office."

"Be careful, Hunt. And if you hear back from your boyfriend, let me know."

"He's not my—" she started to say boyfriend, but the sheriff had already disconnected. Annoyance hit her as she sped down the highway toward the construction office. Dane wouldn't run. He had before, but he wouldn't lie to her. She was almost certain of it.

A few minutes later, she pulled up to the building. There were no other cars in the parking lot. Using a key Dane had loaned her, she quickly let herself in. She hurried upstairs and went straight to the file cabinets. Dane had said Harlan kept hard copies of many documents. She tugged open the top drawer, but everything seemed to be customer information. The employee files were in the third drawer, and she quickly found Alec's. She laid it on the desk and flipped it open.

A scan of the application revealed basic employment history and his home address. Emergency contact information was Nellie Hickman.

Her cell phone buzzed. Silas's name flashed on the screen.

"Did you find Alec?"

"No. There's no one home and the yard is overgrown and his mail looks like it hasn't been picked up in weeks. His curtains are drawn, so I can't see in. If I didn't know he was in town, I'd think the owner had moved out."

"I've been thinking about Layla. What did someone have to gain by hurting her?"

There was a slight pause. "You think they were in a relationship?"

"Yeah, I do. There was someone there the other day when I visited with her. What if they were having a romantic relationship?"

"It's possible."

"I'm worried about Dane. The sheriff suggested he ran again, but I don't believe that. I'm at the construction office. It doesn't look like anyone's been here. Where do you think Alec would take Dane if he has him?"

"I don't know. I'll call the hospital and see if Layla is able to have visitors."

"Okay. I'll let you know if I learn anything." She slid her phone into her back pocket. A glance at Alec's file showed it contained his termination notice. Josie scanned it down to the paragraph that talked about Dane finding Alec drinking in the company's boneyard in a portable office building.

Where was this boneyard? She found Byron Ferguson's, the job foreman, number and called him. He gave her the address to the boneyard.

Would he take Dane there? It'd make sense. On the way out the door, she called Silas, but it went to voicemail, and she left a message. Her next call was to Sheriff Van Carroll.

As she was en route, Bliss called her. Josie gave an update to her boss and let her know where she was headed. She sped down the road. What if he wasn't there? Dane had surprisingly become very important to her.

She didn't know what she would do if something were to happen to him. She simply hadn't planned on him becoming a part of her life again. But he had.

SEVENTEEN

Dane's gaze intensified with Alec's. He didn't want to kill the man, but he was left with no choice. He had to act. As Dane lifted his hand to hit the man's head with the butt of his gun, Alec pulled his trigger.

The bullet whizzed past his shoulder, and as Dane lunged for him, his grip on the gun slipped. His Glock fell to the floorboard.

Alec still held his weapon, so Dane grabbed his wrist and kept his arm wide in case he pulled the trigger again. Like in a game of mercy, both of them held the other while jockeying for position using their bodies as leverage in the pickup.

His opponent's foot wrapped around his thigh, and then they were moving as Alec's foot slipped off the brake. The truck headed into the ditch and picked up speed. "I can't wait to kill you, Haggerty. Even more than Harlan."

No doubt the killer meant his threats. With his left hand, Dane released Alec's arm and went for his throat. His thumb dug into the soft spot to the side of his Adam's apple.

Alec's face turned red, and he cursed.

The truck slammed into something hard, causing them to come to an abrupt stop. They lost their grip on each other, and Alec fired again.

But Dane was too close, and the shot went wild.

His former coworker gritted his teeth and slammed the gun down on the top of Dane's head. Lights danced in his vision, and a loud ringing shouted in his ears.

"Get back to your side of the vehicle." He swiped Dane's Glock from the floorboard and tossed it into the backseat.

Pain radiated throughout his very being as he scooted across the seat.

Alec put the end of his gun barrel up to Dane's temple. "Don't try anything again."

It took incredible effort to open his eyes. The truck was slammed up against the metal railing that kept them from going into a creek. A couple of cars stopped to help, but Alec sped away as one man approached.

A loud racket on the passenger side rang out, making Dane's head hurt even more. The crash must've bent the bumper, causing it to rub against the tire. Against his will, he leaned against the side of the door and closed his eyes. He didn't open them until they made a right turn onto

Miller Lane. The bumpy road was littered with potholes, causing the truck to jolt with each hit.

A mile later, Alec turned into a drive on the left.

The company's boneyard. The place contained old equipment that needed to be repaired and a surplus of building supplies. What was Alec's plan? Thankfully, Josie didn't know about his place so she wouldn't look here for him. He wanted her far away from this madman.

As he forced his eyes to stay open against the pain, he sought a way to escape. The large pile of metal and other materials were a blur as they whizzed past. He'd been meaning to organize the boneyard months prior to Harlan's death but had never found the time. He tried to remember what else was stored there.

The truck stopped in front of a portable office—the same metal building where Dane had caught Alec drinking and that had cost him his job.

"Get out." Alec waved his gun at him. "Don't try anything if you want to see Josie again."

As much as Dane wanted to rebel, he withheld the urge. Moisture ran across his head, telling him the hit from the gun had caused him to bleed. The ringing had lessened, but he still didn't feel at the top of his game. If Alec had wanted to kill him, surely he could've done so on the road and left his body in a ditch.

His boots hit the dirt.

"Do you have any other weapons on you?" Alec came up behind him and quickly patted him down. He poked him in the back with the gun. "Move inside."

Dane held his hands out in full view and did as he was asked. When he entered the small structure, it took a moment for his eyes to adjust.

"Sit." Alec waved his pistol in the direction of a ripped office chair. A small chain looped in and out through the chair's frame and was bolted to the leg of the desk.

He had no sooner sat down than Alec withdrew two long zip ties from his back pocket. Grabbing him roughly, he attached his wrist to the arm. Dane didn't put up a fight. He tried to keep his arm away from the metal arm to give him wiggle room, but Alec clamped it tight, the tie biting into his flesh.

"You can't get away with this."

"I have so far. No one connects me to you." Alec grinned big. He moved in front of him and leaned down so that Dane had no choice but to look at him. "The sheriff's department is looking for you and only you. I was so exhilarated when you ran, making you look even more guilty. As soon as Josie and Everly get here, you'll be blamed for their deaths, too. You know, it really doesn't matter if I kill you now or later, I can position your body however I want to make it look like you killed them, but Josie got off one shot. It's not that difficult. Some of the fun would be diminished, because I'd like for you to suffer."

Dane's blood thumped through his ears, angry that anyone could be so heartless. But most of all, fear of losing Josie drove him the most. Just when he'd started believing in the system and people and that he could have a chance at a good life again. One he intended to show Violet, and maybe his mom, if she'd let him. So many good things at his fingertips and this man could ruin everything.

Not if Dane could help it. At least if Alec was here, that meant Josie was safe for the moment.

Tires on the drive sounded outside. He recognized the sound of Josie's Bronco.

He didn't know if Alec heard it or not, but Dane had to do something.

Alec's cell phone dinged. The man moved to the door and turned to look at Dane with a smile. "I have a little surprise for you."

Josie noted the silver GMC which she concluded must belong to Alec was parked in front of a metal building. She pulled to the corner of the property behind a small dozer type of equipment called a skid steer.

She was confident that Sheriff Van Carroll and Texas Ranger Boone both should be on their way. She checked her gun and then quietly exited her vehicle. She eased around the piles of building materials, from metal beams to ceramic tile, and moved to the side of the portable building. Indecision as to whether she should enter to see how Dane was making out or wait for backup warred within her.

She decided on the safest route. Even though Dane had never been in law enforcement, he had a canny survival mode. Before she could settle in somewhere that hid her while giving her a good view of the building, the door swung open, and Alec strode out.

Although she'd never met the man, she realized Everly had done a great job describing his features. For an eight-year-old, she'd recalled Alec's characteristics better than Josie could've.

She watched the murderer and noted the grin tugging on his mouth. Disgust bit into her as she wondered if he'd hurt Dane. Remaining calm was essential. She couldn't panic like she had the day her family had perished.

Suddenly, dust lifted in the distance as a vehicle came toward them. She hoped it was the Texas Ranger. As the vehicle grew closer, she realized the beat-up black truck looked familiar. It was the same one that chased them through the quarry.

Alec's head turned directly to where she was hiding, causing her to back up. Had he seen her? She chanced a glance around the corner to see a smug expression on his face.

He knew she was there. But why hadn't Dane come out of the building?

Alec stepped toward the car and a man got out of the driver's door. She saw that it was Phillip from the retirement home. Then Alec opened the back door and pulled Everly out of the vehicle. Then he looked across the yard to her.

Josie's heart stopped. "Let her go!"

Everly's head came up and their eyes locked. "Mom!"

Her heart hitched at the fear in her daughter's face. Everly's hair was tussled, making Josie wonder if the girl had put up a fight.

Alec tugged Everly's hand and dragged her toward the building even though her feet dug into the gravel, and she sank back almost until her bottom was on the ground. Alec called, "You can join us inside now, Miss Hunt."

With her gun still in her hand, she ran across the property, weaving in and out of the piles of junk and got to the door at the same time as they did. "Let her go."

Alec clucked his tongue and shook his head. "You know I can't do that." His eyebrows shot up and he waved the weapon in his hand. "Drop your weapon unless you want the girl to die right here."

Josie did as she was asked.

The man shoved the door open and stepped inside with her daughter. Josie turned to Phillip. "I can't believe you helped Alec with this."

"Sorry, Josie. It was nothing personal." He shrugged. "My cousin needed help and I didn't want to turn him down. Sometimes a person needs money, and at my age, there's not many opportunities." Phillip was Alec's cousin? She'd had no idea. The man actually looked ashamed, but she had no sympathy. A person made choices. "Your grandpa was not hurt, if it's any consolation. I can't say the same for that psychologist lady."

Kennedy. Josie said a quick prayer her friend was not hurt. If what he said was true, she'd check on her grandfather and Kennedy as soon as she could. When she stepped inside the small building, she caught sight of Dane lying on the floor as if he'd tried to break free and fell, his wrists tied to a chair that was chained to the desk. His jaw twitched as defeat showed in his eyes.

"You can leave now, Phillip. Shut the door behind you."

The orderly hesitated, his gaze shifting to Josie. Then he walked out.

Josie hurried over to Dane and helped get his chair back to an upright position. Their eyes collided and in that moment, she thought Dane would kill Alec if given the opportunity.

"Let my daughter go, Alec."

He shook his head and pulled Everly against

him. "Can't do that. She's seen too much. Now, get over there." He indicated the corner with his gun.

"No." She and Dane exchanged glances again and this time she detected something in his eyes. He had a plan. She didn't understand what it was, but at this point, she'd try anything. She looked up at Alec. "Whatever you intend to do, you need to rethink the situation."

Dane's gaze went to the window, telling her someone was out there. She hoped it was the sheriff. When he looked back to her, he nodded big. She ducked.

Dane swept out with his boot, kicking Alec in the leg.

The door burst open. Silas stood in the doorway with his gun drawn.

"Silas Boone, Texas Ranger. Drop your weapon."

Alec lay on the floor, and his face turned red. Instead of doing as he was told, he gave a loud yell, and his hand came up with his gun.

Silas pulled the trigger, shooting Alec once in the shoulder. The killer's gun fell to the floor. After the Ranger retrieved it, Bliss hurried through the door to Josie. "Are you okay?"

"Yeah, I think so." She turned to Everly and held her arms out. Her daughter flung herself against her, crying. Josie inhaled an emotional breath as she clung to her for several moments.

Silas cut Dane's restraints with a pocketknife, freeing him.

Finally, Josie let go of Everly and pulled back to look her in the face. "Are you all right? Did the man hurt you?"

Her face wrinkled into a frown. "I'm okay." She pointed at Alec. "He killed my daddy."

"I know, baby. I know." If she could, Josie would undo time and go back to help save Pierce from this man. "He'll be going to prison for a long time."

Deputy Hattie Perkins came through the door and slapped handcuffs on Hickman. She talked into her radio and asked for paramedics.

They all backed up to give the deputy room as she escorted Alec out of the room and into the back of her SUV. Needing air, Josie took Everly outside the stuffy building.

Dane strode over to her, his eyes full of concern. "Are you certain you two are okay?"

"I think so. And you?"

"I'm good now. Alec rammed into the back of my motorcycle when I was on the way to visit the sheriff." He nodded. "I'm glad this is over."

"Haggerty." Sheriff Van Carroll's voice traveled across the parking lot.

"Maybe I spoke too soon." He turned to the lawman. "Sheriff."

Josie moved forward. "Sheriff, Dane was on

his way to turn himself in when Alec Hickman, the real killer, kidnapped him."

"I've got this," Dane whispered before continuing the conversation with Van Carroll. "I shouldn't have run, but I was afraid I'd be arrested and not get a fair trial."

The sheriff folded his arms across his chest as Dane gave the short version of what had happened months ago through today when Alec brought him to the boneyard.

"I'll need you to come by the department and fill out a statement. You will still be investigated, but if you're clean, all charges will be dropped."

"I'm clean." Dane walked back to Josie and pulled her hands into hers. "I never could've done this without you."

"I told you to trust in the system."

A smile tugged at his mouth. "Easier said than done." His gaze stayed with hers like there was something he wanted to say but was hesitant. Everly stood close to him, and his arm went to her shoulder.

Josie stared at him. "What is it?"

"I'd like to stay in touch."

Somehow that's not the words she'd hoped to hear. "In touch? Like friends on social media? Or maybe the occasional visit over coffee?"

He took a step back before running his hands through his hair. "You know I'm not good at expressing myself, but I want more." He waved his hand between her and him. "Of this. Us."

Everly looked up at him. "Does that include me?"

Josie smiled, and he laughed.

"Of course, it does." Dane grew serious as he turned to Josie. "Since the day I met you, you've been important to me. I'd like you back in my life. You make me a better man. I love you."

Her spirits lifted. "It's going to take some time to sort through this, but I love you, too."

"Mom, I like him."

Josie smiled. "I know you do. Me, too. He's a good man."

EPILOGUE

"Mom. Help me!"

Josie glanced up to see Everly running around a tree with Violet in hot pursuit. Dexter barked excitedly as he danced around them.

As Violet touched her, she yelled, "You're it."

"Oh, come on," Everly complained. "You had a head start."

"Nuh-uh. I just took a shortcut. Besides, I had Wyatt with me."

Josie brought the tray of marshmallows, chocolate bars, and graham crackers out the back door. Dane sat beside the campfire straightening several wire coat hangers. "Here you go."

They were gathered at Dane's home in the country. Already, plans were in the works to add another bedroom to give each of the girls a room of their own.

All of the families of Bring Home the Children Project team were gathered around the campfire.

Josie couldn't have been happier. Dane had been exonerated of all charges. Of course, she knew he would. They married last month, just two months after Alec Hickman had been arrested.

Alec received life in prison without the possibility for parole for killing Pierce and Harlan, a plea deal that kept him from a trial where he might have received the death penalty. Layla turned in evidence against Alec to avoid jail time. She admitted after being pursued for months, she finally had an affair with Alec and began taking money from the business behind her husband's back. But Alec pressured her to leave Harlan. Ultimately, she agreed, and they planned to take a long vacation in Mexico, and they would live off the divorce settlement. But when she hesitated to steal thirty thousand dollars, Alec went behind her back and withdrew the money from the account. Alec often snooped while his mom cleaned the offices, and he found a receipt that showed Pierce had been hired to investigate him. Believing it had to do with the missing money, he approached Harlan to proclaim his innocence, but the owner informed him he knew of the affair. Alec went into a rage and killed Harlan and set up Dane to take the fall. Realizing the investigator could tie Alec to Harlan, he was forced to kill him, too.

Once Layla realized how much Alec despised Harlan and Dane for firing him, it was too late.

She was afraid to go against him, but in the end, he attacked her anyway.

Except for the occasional argument, Violet and Everly had become best friends instantly. Even before the wedding, Kennedy had counseled their family, which mostly was intended to help the girls. Josie was surprised how much talking about her past and the fire had helped her to see things more clearly. It was common for victims of tragedy to feel guilt for being a survivor. Her main regret was not seeking counseling earlier. Even Dane claimed he'd learned a lot about himself and was glad to have participated.

The kids gathered around while the men assisted in loading the wires with marshmallows to hang over the flames. The women finished carrying out the snacks.

Bliss smiled. "This get-together was a great idea. Wyatt loves the great outdoors. He and Spencer have really gotten to be close friends."

Kennedy brought out a pitcher of lemonade. Thankfully she was not injured when Phillip abducted Everly from the retirement home. He'd pulled a gun on her and then locked her in the medication storage closet.

Silas got up and took the lemonade from her. "I've got this."

A yellow Jeep pulled up and Annie and Riggs Brenner climbed out with a baby, two women and a man. Josie hurried over to Annie. "I'm so glad you all could make it. I know it's a long drive from Palo Duro Canyon."

Annie smiled. "It is. Especially with a teething six-month-old baby."

"Oh, can I hold her?"

"Certainly. Josie, meet Kelsey." The adorable girl had lots of dark hair and a stream of drool running down her chin. "And you remember Tami."

Josie had helped Annie and Riggs with a case in West Texas. Not only had they found and brought two children to their parents, but Annie had been reunited with Tami, who'd been abducted many years earlier. Annie promised she'd help Tami find her missing sister. The woman had changed a lot since Josie had last seen her. She'd gained weight and appeared healthier.

"This is my sister, Casey, and her husband, Jake."

"Glad to meet you." With the precious baby in her arms, Josie followed them to the campfire where Annie introduced them to everyone. Recently Annie learned Casey had been adopted in New Mexico by an older couple. Annie found Casey by using a family genealogy website. The funny thing was, Casey had been searching for Tami for years, but since her DNA wasn't in the system, she hadn't been able to find her.

An arm went around Josie's waist, and she

looked up into Dane's glistening eyes. "This was a great idea, honey."

She searched his face. "It's not too much? I realize you don't know many of my team members very well, and meeting new people—"

He placed his finger on her lips and shook his head. "I like them. I can't help but think that Harlan would've enjoyed their company, too."

"From everything you've told me about him, I can see that. Are you ready to roast the marshmallows?"

"First—" Dane leaned in, his warm breath on her cheek "—I need one more of these." He planted a kiss on her lips.

She playfully slapped his shoulder. "You have a lifetime of those."

"It won't be nearly enough."

* * * * *

If you liked this story from Connie Queen,
check out her previous
Love Inspired Suspense books:

Justice Undercover
Texas Christmas Revenge
Canyon Survival
Abduction Cold Case
Tracking the Tiny Target
Rescuing the Stolen Child

Available now from Love Inspired Suspense!
Find more great reads at LoveInspired.com.

Dear Reader,

Thank you for reading *Wilderness Witness Survival*.

In the story, Josie recently adopted a girl, and Dane would like to adopt his sister. Kids, foster care and adoption are something near and dear to my heart. (Even though sometimes in fiction, foster care makes an easy target. Sorry.) Caring for any child can be difficult, but being a parent to someone's child who carries baggage from the past can present unique challenges. To all parents, whether you're raising your home-grown kids, or starting in the middle of a child's journey, your job is the most important in the world. Remember, to look to God for answers.

I hope you enjoyed the Bring the Children Home Project stories. I thoroughly enjoyed writing them.

I love to hear from readers! You can connect with me at conniequeenauthor.com or on my Facebook page.

Connie Queen